IN SALEM, MASSACHUSETTS, during the 1690s, "innocent" young girls set off a massive witchhunt. Are they the suffering victims or the Devil's tools?

IN MIAMI, FLORIDA, a teenager's room explodes with eerie noises and other strange manifestations. Is it a poltergeist or the girl's own mental projections?

IN TAHITI, a small boy is shunned by the islanders as a creature of the demon god Tu, when those who oppose the child mysteriously die. Is it just coincidence or a case of possession?

IN ILLINOIS, a thirteen-year-old girl is invaded by the spirit of an older girl and recalls the most intimate details of the dead girl's life. Is it telepathy or true spiritual contact?

These are just a few of the incredible but true cases that will give you a shocking new view of a phenomenon that could happen to any family, anywhere, at any time. . . .

DEMON CHILDREN

DEMON
CHILDREN

Edited by
Martin Ebon

A SIGNET BOOK
NEW AMERICAN LIBRARY
TIMES MIRROR

Permissions Acknowledgments

"God, the Devil, and Little David," by Rick Anderson, originally appeared in *The Seattle Post–Intelligencer*, November 21, 1976. Copyright © 1976 by *The Seattle Post–Intelligencer*. Reprinted by permission.

"Never Again!" by Martin Ebon, originally appeared under the title "Seaford Revisited: Post-Mortem on a Poltergeist" in *Tomorrow*, Summer 1958. Copyright © 1958 by Garrett Publications. Reprinted by permission.

"Murder of the Child Witch," by Paul Langdon, originally appeared under the title "Twentieth-Century Victim" in *Witchcraft Today*, an anthology edited by Martin Ebon. Copyright © 1971 by Lombard Associates, Inc. Reprinted by arrangement with The New American Library, Inc., New York, N.Y.

SIGNET, SIGNET CLASSICS, MENTOR, PLUME AND MERIDIAN BOOKS
are published by The New American Library, Inc.,
1301 Avenue of the Americas, New York, New York 10019

FIRST SIGNET PRINTING, MARCH, 1978

1 2 3 4 5 6 7 8 9

PRINTED IN THE UNITED STATES OF AMERICA

CONTENTS

forces within them were successfully exorcised, but one boy died two years after this experience, and the other was able to survive only a brief life span. Family and priests were convinced that the two boys had been truly possessed by the Devil. 131

1. INTRODUCTION: A Mask for Evil

Martin Ebon

Suddenly, our society has discovered ancient evil behind a modern mask: demon possession of a child. In a macabre kaleidoscope of motion pictures, novels, child beatings, and sexual abuse of the young, a new diabolical image has been created. Behind a variety of disguises, we encounter a repelling psychological reality: fascination with demonic lust and abuse, imposed on an innocent girl or boy.

On the following pages, a series of factual reports on "possession" of children will be presented. They cover different times and places, but share the underlying theme of demonic manipulation from behind the most unlikely masks, the body and soul of a child or teen-age youngster. The theme is as old as man's written records. We learn from the Gospel of Mark (10:10) that Christ was approached by a man who said, "Master, I brought my son to you. He is possessed by a spirit which makes him speechless. Whenever it attacks him, it throws him to the ground, and he foams at the mouth, grinds his teeth, and goes rigid." The disciples had tried to oust the entity from the boy, but it had resisted successfully. Now Jesus himself observed that the spirit "threw the boy into convulsions," so that he "fell to the ground and rolled about foaming at the mouth." Diabolic or demon possession, or possession by an "evil" or "unclean" spirit were used interchangeably in early Christian writings; it has remained that way, in many cases, to this day.

When Christ saw the boy suffering, he asked his father, "How long has he been like this?" The father told him that the boy had suffered these attacks since childhood; often, he added, the possessing entity had tried to kill him "by throwing him into the fire or water." He pleaded with Jesus

1

and said, "But if it is at all possible for you, take pity upon us and help us." To this, Jesus replied reassuringly, "It is possible! Everything is possible to one who has faith." The father cried out, "I have faith; help me where faith falls short."

Then, while the crowd of the awed and curious milled about, Christ "rebuked" the demon and said, "Deaf and dumb spirit, I command you, come out of him, and never go back." This phrase has remained a key to religious exorcisms to this day. According to the Gospel of Mark, the possessing entity at first cried aloud and racked the boy's body "fiercely," but finally gave up and "came out." The boy remained on the ground, unmoving, and some of the onlookers said, "He is dead." But "Jesus took his hand and raised him to his feet, and he stood up."

The image of the demon-possessed child is doubly dramatic, because a young girl or boy has an undeveloped identity, something relatively easily controlled by a nonhuman entity. This theme, that of a child acting as a mere shell for the personality and destructive schemes of another entity, permeates the images which novels and motion pictures have conveyed in recent years. The mastery of evil over innocence, at least temporarily, has captured the imagination of readers and film audiences throughout the world.

But while one can put down a book or leave a motion picture theater with the reassuring feeling that it is "all made up," that is not the case with the material presented in this volume. True, it is human language that speaks of devils, demons, and evil spirits. True, too, today's knowledge of psychology enables us to use more clinical labels than "demon possession." But we are experiencing a renewal of serious interest in established religious concepts, and the themes we encounter in fiction, films, and on television have counterparts in a number of strong contemporary religious movements.

Diabolic possession, calling for exorcism by a priestly exorcist, is most firmly established in the Roman Catholic Church, where the rites were clearly defined in the *Rituale Romanum*, published in Rome in 1614. But the Anglican and Episcopal churches practice similar rites, as do a number of Protestant denominations. The phenomenon of possession is cross-cultural. It can be found in virtually all parts of the world. Its presence can be traced to ancient China; in Babylon, cuneiform tablets enable us to find evidence of possession and exorcism beliefs some 5,000 to 6,000 years ago.

As if the very idea of demon possession of an innocent child were not macabre enough, current interest in this theme shows a sinister relation to other adult involvement with young boys and girls. What we encounter in this area is filled with hidden or open elements of hostility and sexual depravity. This cauldron of adult-child interrelation ranges from murder to beating and torturing, sexual abuse, the filming and photographing of intercourse between adults and children, sexual contact between children, as well as incest, notably between fathers (including stepfathers) and daughters.

Fear and hate are major ingredients of this cauldron. So far, psychologists have not managed to sort them out. But the time is obviously approaching when we will obtain a clearer picture of how adults truly feel about children, including their own, and this may well bear little resemblance to the sugarcoated images we have inherited from generations before us. A preliminary exploration of "Demoniacal Possession and Childhood Purity," by Dr. Benjamin Beit-Hallahmi, appeared in the *American Imago,* a psychoanalytic quarterly (Fall 1976); the author attributes public fascination with these themes to "their ability to echo and fathom our own impulses." Evil, he says, is equivalent to "our own unacceptable impulses." What we'd like to do ourselves, according to this school of psychology, we "project" on others: we paint them with the brush of our own destructive, demeaning, socially improper wishes and desires. As Dr. Beit-Hallahmi puts it, "The most common solution to the problem of reconciling our unacceptable impulses and our positive self images is by projection. We project the evil in us on demons, devils, ghosts, witches, in-laws, and just plain people."

He forgot to add: children. Because, by now, it looks as if at least our novelists and film makers have discovered a most unlikely vehicle for our hatreds and lusts, the young and innocent. Stories and movies reveal elements in our nation's character, and in the whole world's unraveling psyche, about as much as do our individual dreams or personal fantasies. But everyday reality is brutal enough. The sexual abuse and murder of the young has now surfaced with blatant savagery. It is not limited to the big cities, whose centers are often called an "urban jungle."

Take, as an example, the events that shocked the town of Birmingham, Michigan, an affluent suburb of Detroit in 1976 and 1977. Although the mass killings of children in Birmingham were obviously the deeds of what the newspapers call "a psychopathic killer," they merely reflect the extremes of a trend that has either been growing stronger or has surfaced most dramatically at the present time. In the Birmingham case, boys and girls, from ten to sixteen years in age, were murdered by a killer who committed his crime only during snowstorms, scrubbed and cleaned the bodies, and laid them out in the snow as if ready for a coffin.

The Birmingham killer started his one-man crime wave in January 1976, and more than a year later he had still not been caught. His first victim was sixteen-year-old Cynthia Cadieux, who had walked home from a girl friend's house on the fifteenth of the month at 8:30 P.M. Five hours later, her nude body was found displayed in the snow. The second victim was a boy, Mark Stebbins. The fifteen-year-old youngster had been playing outside an American Legion Hall. He had been strangled, undressed, washed, his fingernails cleaned, his hair combed, and then dressed again. He had been sexually abused.

Thirteen-year-old Jane Louise Allan was found near the Great Miami River. She had been bound and clothed. Her death was attributed to carbon monoxide poisoning. Jill Robinson, thirteen years old, was abducted on her way home from the Tiny Tim Hobby Center on December 22, 1976. She was apparently alive over the Christmas holidays, but killed with a shotgun on December 26. Evidence showed that she had been bathed before her death.

The sixth victim in the series was ten-year-old Christine Minelich, abducted on her way home four days after the Robinson killing. It took eighteen days to find her body, strangled, washed, neatly dressed, and laid out on a snow bank. Eleven-year-old Timothy King disappeared from a local supermarket in Birmingham. Apparently he was well cared for and properly fed for several days. But, finally, he was choked to death. He, too, had been bathed. Even his clothes had been cleaned. He had been placed carefully, in the ritual of the killer, in a snow bank. His body was still warm when found by a police patrol.

With talk of demoniacal influences in the air, it is easy enough to speculate that the killer himself may be under the control of a demonic spirit. The odd ritual used by the killer—his compulsive cleanliness—may suggest that he psychopathically believes that he is assuring their purity by killing them at an age of innocence, even protecting them against the depravity of contemporary civilization. The presence of white snow, symbol of pristine purity, reinforces this deranged but oddly consistent train of thought.

The Birmingham cases merely illustrate a nationwide trend of alarming proportions. Estimates, which obviously cannot be completely accurate, now state that close to 200,000 children are killed by their guardians each year. The number of children who are "only" beaten and battered yearly is somewhere around 2 million. The tendency to project upon children the frustrations of the parents—like blaming misfortune on demons or spells in primitive societies—is clearly evident. An educational film, designed to alert parents who vent their frustrations on helpless offspring, shows a father returning from work, with money troubles on his mind, finding the television set out of order. After urging his young son to remove his toy trains from the living room several times, he throws himself on the child in a fit of rage and punches him mercilessly.

I believe that the high incidence of child murders and child abuse are related to the pervasive and macabre attraction of the general public for tales of the demon-possession of children. Adults are thus able to project their own darkly hidden desires on the most helpless and innocent of humans: children. Legal concepts make children under age, for all practical purposes, the "property" of their parents or guardians. They can, in effect, do with them whatever they like. The machinery for bringing the fate of a brutally abused baby to the attention of public authorities is severely handicapped by legal procedures. Even doctors and nurses who are fully aware that an infant, brought to a hospital after a supposed "accident," is clearly the victim of assault with a blunt instrument, are reluctant to press charges. They tend to engage in a game of make-believe of superficial acceptance of the parents-guardians' transparent efforts to hide the criminal abuse of their own offspring.

It is in this atmosphere that the concept of the demon child has flourished. Parents are only too ready, consciously or unconsciously, to see the child as "bad," unreasonable, and ill behaved to the point of evil, and even—given a specific religiocultural attitude—as an instrument controlled by the Devil. Janet Chase Marshall, writing in the monthly *Human Behavior* (March 1977), has discussed the subject "Children of the Devil" in the light of current trends. She proposes that the very parents who educated their children according to liberal concepts prevalent in the 1960s, gave them all advantages, "made the best sort of role models," and "never laid an angry hand on them" have discovered that it was all in vain.

Instead, Miss Marshall writes that "these fictional parents" of current literature and movies "produced a litter of antichrists, witches, assorted demons, reincarnated changelings and pathological murderers." The theme of "the innocent child as a battleground for the struggle between good and evil," she found has new "mass appeal." Martin D. Widzer, M.D., assistant clinical professor of psychiatry at the University of California, Los Angeles, believes that this concept allows us to project outward our fears that we are just cogs in an uncaring universe, that no matter how hard we try to do well by our kids, ultimately we have little control over them."

It is Dr. Widzer's conclusion that it helps the individual if he can "project that helplessness out to something else—to the devil, for instance. But you can't attach your fantasies to anything with too much structure, because reality would get in the way. It is easier to attach them to a child . . ."

A similar view is held by a Los Angeles psychologist, Ann Alpern, who says that "a lot of parents cannot accept any responsibility for hostility between their children and themselves. It makes them feel upset with themselves and betrayed by their children. They don't teach their children how to work with anger; so the kids feel their anger is abnormal, and they don't know what to do with it."

If that is so, what kind of emotional release is achieved by people who read the book or see the movie *The Omen*, or *Carrie*, or *Audrey Rose*? What good does all this gory horror do to people who look at it on the movie screen? Alpern says that seeing the child as "evil or possessed is one way of working through these feelings." She finds that parents experience quite contradictory emotions when watching the sort of movie which pictures an apparently totally innocent child as a victim of demon possession. In fact, she notes that the adults experience "some satisfaction in seeing the child get hurt. On the other hand, this child is someone valuable and, to some extent, an extension of yourself."

In the movies and novels that deal with demon possession, reincarnation, and other occult subjects, the parents are almost invariably pictured as affluent, well-educated people who run just about as ideal a household as can be pictured in fantasies nurtured by the media. In *The Omen*, the father (played with dignity by Gregory Peck) is U.S. ambassador to the Court of St. James (London) who discovers that his little boy is the Antichrist. In *Audrey Rose* (where a stranger claims a child as the reincarnation of his own dead daughter, and wants her back), the parents are upper-class, active intellectuals who live an enviable, well-heeled existence.

Dr. Widzer has an explanation of why authors and moviemakers cast the parents of the occult-beset children as "princes and princesses" in our society. He believes that their position "provides a distance, so that people can grasp the content of a story without getting overwhelmed. In addition, it fulfills a wish to snoop on people." And author Marshall thinks "we probably also derive some degree of pleasure in seeing the 'fancy' people getting taken down a notch or two." Alpern sees the possessed child as a mere "thing," while "the real conflict is the devil versus the parent."

The fictional versions of diabolic or demonic intrusion coincide with the current wave of child pornography, incest, sexual depravity, and murder; Janet Chase Marshall sees it this way: "Beneath all the wide-eyed innocence, these stories are absolutely spilling over with images of sensuality." The prepubescent period is one of a mixture between neuter innocence and the promise of a ripening toward sexual maturity. Intimations of a tempting-teasing femininity could be found in earlier child stars. Back in 1936, British novelist Graham Greene reviewed Shirley Temple's performance in *Captain January*, saying, "Her popularity seems to rest on a coquetry quite as mature as Miss [Claudette] Colbert and on an oddly precocious body as voluptuous in gray flannel trousers as Miss [Marlene] Dietrich's."

But a vast chasm separates the Shirley Temple image from the exploitation of young girls in today's films, quite aside from the sleazy pornographic productions. One "kiddie porn" magazine calls itself *Lollitos,* a name that conjures up images of tiny tots and lollipops, at the same time evoking Vladimir Nabokov's novel *Lolita,* which centered on a mature man's seduction of a girl child. We now encounter such types as the child prostitute played by Jody Foster in *Taxi Driver*, a movie built around the psychopathic fantasies and crimes of an urban paranoiac.

It should be clear from all the foregoing that current fascinations with the "demon child" theme touches the lower depths of human emotions, where commercial exploitation meets the depraved and the criminal. The colloquialisms of this trade would be amusing, if they weren't so fundamentally tragic. Urban areas where preadolescent boys and girls display their bodies in pool rooms or pinball joints, or just out in the street, are called "meat markets." Mature men who go hunting for under-age prostitutes are known as "chicken hawks." Peddlers of porno films of prepubescent girls refer to their merchandise as "Bald Pussy."

Underlying these depravities is a pervasive change in attitude toward the very young. Small wonder many religious spokesmen anticipate that our civilization is moving toward a final cataclysm, to an Apocalypse that will wipe out these demonic aberrations; the tolerant rulings on obscenity, handed down by the U.S. Supreme Court, and their application by local law enforcement agencies, bear a heavy responsibility for this cultural aberration.

The "demon child" has become a concept in which a pseudoreligious resurgence joins forces with a new hatred and fear of the young. And yet, as we see on the following pages, diabolic possession and exorcism of children and young teenagers can be found in virtually all times and places. There is a universal attraction for the demon possession of the young innocent that creates an almost irresistible cauldron of terror and fascination.

2. God, the Devil, and Little David

Rick Anderson

It was clear to Leon Cunningham that three-year-old David was possessed by the Devil. Citing the biblical phrase, from Proverbs, ". . . for if thou beatest him with a rod he shall not die" and "thou shalt deliver his soul from hell," the family began to take turns in beating little David Weilbacher. This all took place in Yakima, Washington, in late 1976. Cunningham also engaged in a form of exorcism of whatever demonic entity might be inhabiting the child; he called his actions "humblings," and they consisted in pushing the little boy to the floor, urging him to get up, and beating him if he did not rise. One day he did not get up, ever again. Yet, Cunningham and the other members of his household expected David to "arise." After two months, a police sergeant entered the room in which the body had been kept. Rick Anderson, who covered the trial of the family members, is a member of the editorial staff of The Seattle Post-Intelligencer.

David Weilbacher, named for his father, was a big-eyed, dark blond, handsome boy of two years when his mother brought him to the house on South 12th Street in Yakima, Washington. The old yellow building with chocolate trim and tile roof is set back on a narrow lot in a neighborhood of crumbling streets, dirt alleys and one-room shacks, a ghetto of dust and poverty on Yakima's southeast side. It was not much as a place to live, and absolutely no place to die.

Debra Marie Weilbacher, 19 when she began taking David to the yellow house each day last September, was an Army brat, born in Fort Benning, Georgia, later moving with her family to Utah and then Washington. On March 25, 1972, 16-year-old Debbie dropped out of school and got married.

On January 4 of the following year her only child was born. But the marriage was already failing. Debbie and her Marine husband spent only two months out of the four years together. Two weeks after little David's third birthday, their divorce was final.

By then, Debbie and little David had moved out of their small Yakima apartment and into the old yellow house on South 12th. Debbie had been told about it by a former schoolmate, Lorraine Edwards, whom Debbie had sought out. Lonely, empty, Debbie was turning towards religion. Someone told her Lorraine knew of a family who might help her. One day in early September, 1975, Lorraine invited her to the house. Debbie's reaction was immediate. She felt loved. She wanted badly to return. It was not just a house, but a church, with a family whose existence revolved around the Bible and God. The next time Debbie came back, she gave herself to Him. In a ceremonial rite presided over by the head of the family, Debbie was saved. She was also worried.

If I go back out into the world, I won't make it, Debra Weilbacher thought then. *I'll be a sinner again.*

She asked the family if she could move in with them. By December, the family had grown by two. Debra and David were not only close to God, but lived with a man through whom He spoke. Edward Leon Cunningham, 51, told her God was his master, and he was God's messenger.

Edward Leon Cunningham came out of Oklahoma, as did his wife, Velma, but they didn't meet until their paths crossed in California over 30 years ago. Velma was not long out of grade school, Leon just out of his teens. When they wed, 12 days into the New Year of 1946, Leon was 21, Velma was 14. The following November, she was also a mother, giving birth to the first of seven children.

Leon, for years, was a heavy drinker, gambler and sinner, particularly during his rowdy Army days. He once won $88 on a $2 bet and never forgot it. His little bit of money was often thrown after this illusion, even through the first nine years of marriage to Velma Geraldine Cunningham, a slightly-built girl bearing a mild resemblance to the character actress popular in those days, Thelma Ritter.

But Leon was unhappy with himself then. Neither of them were serious church-goers and there seemed no meaning to their lives. In the mid-50's, however, Leon began to change. His father, like his grandfather, was a solid Baptist. They called themselves ministers. Leon's father urged his son to turn again to the God he had forgotten. The change, at first, was gradual. Then dramatic. One day, two years later, Leon heard God's voice. Later, when Leon spoke, it was as if God himself was speaking through Leon. It was then, over 20 years ago, that Leon, like his father and his grandfather, became a minister. He inspired his children to follow.

Occasionally, Leon, a stubby, overweight man with wiry, short, gray hair and a scarlet rashlike condition on his right cheek and tip of his nose, would speak at churches, delivering casual sermons. Mostly, however, he ministered at home, to his family, raising them in a spiritual world dedicated to God, dictated by the Bible and, specifically, defending all against the devil. Leon knew about the devil. He had seen it once, at least, in his children, in Marilyn the second-oldest. Through ritualistic prayer, the demon was driven from her.

Years later, however, it would take much more than prayer to exorcise the devil from the house on South 12th Street.

Other family and friends kept the house full, and at times crowded, through last winter and spring, the seventh in Yakima for the Cunninghams. At times, there were nine or ten people staying in the wood-frame house of four bedrooms, kitchen and living room. But the principal family was composed of Debbie, Leon, and Velma and their one unmarried daughter, Carolyn, 27, a large, square-faced woman who dropped out of school after the 8th grade; Lorraine, who had joined after giving birth to a son fathered by one of Leon's sons—who later married another woman who lived for a while at the house. And of course there was David.

When the family looks back, it is not sure when the change came over David, exactly. He had seemed a normal boy but not particularly friendly with other children, although he had spent most of his years growing up around adults.

Leon, however, was the first to notice it, sometime in the spring, after the girls had taken David with them on a stroll around the neighborhood, passing the shells of three burned-out houses.

At home later, while his mother was fixing food in the kitchen, David seemed to babble about the houses. They seemed to fascinate David, whose grandfather was a fireman. The boy's talk of the houses stuck in Leon's mind. Previously,

Leon had been concerned about other things, including the end of the nonspiritual world again.

Leon, a sometimes car salesman, mechanic and odd-jobber, had gotten visions on other occasions that led him to pick possible dates when an anti-Christ would arise and destroy all those who failed to believe as Leon believed. On Nov 22, 1975, the 12th anniversary of President John F. Kennedy's assassination, a spiritual change swept through the household. That was when Leon had received his vision the anti-Christ, who would arise August 18 this year, would be John F. Kennedy reincarnate. Other members of the family had their own visions, one seeing a barn, another a farm. Leon saw Texas. Eventually, the picture was a Texas farm where the family would be safe from Kennedy. In December, they began selling their household goods and other property to pay for the move. Leon ended up with $1,700 cash.

The family's thoughts, their habits, their lives revolved around God and the Bible as told by Leon. They also held twice-a-week services open to anyone, and occasionally strangers would drift in. The neighbors heard the gospel singing, saw the family about the house, but paid little attention. The family paid attention only to one of the neighbors' truck, a shack built onto the back of it, which would be perfect for their escape to Texas. Without their TV and furniture, living frugally—including canceling their newspaper subscription after God told Leon if there was anything to know God would inform them—the family prepared for the move. Except now, there was this problem with David.

It took some months, but the family began to add it all up. Leon pointed things out to them: first the burned-out houses. It just wasn't right for a child to act that way. Then David's attitude, wetting his pants, smearing his waste on the bathroom wall. He smelled wicked, too, for some unknown reason. Once he put glass chips in his shoes and wore them. David acted like he would rather be an adult than a child, although he had a laugh, a foolish laugh, that seemed to be neither young nor old. And there was the cough, something he would seem to work up all by himself. It kept his mother awake at night, on purpose it appeared, and once she remembers waking up suddenly because she felt David had bitten her on the shoulder. She finally had to make him sleep in a room by himself after she found him staring at her in the mornings. In the end, it was clear, particularly to Leon. David Weilbacher, age 3, was possessed by the devil.

The spankings began in April, the family remembers. Leon had pointed to something in the Bible which he believed was the answer. It was out of Proverbs: "Withhold not correction from the child: for if thou beatest him with a rod he shall not die. Thou shalt deliver his soul from hell."

They could beat David. They could, twice a day with David in his underwear, beat David to drive the devil out of him and David would not die. The Bible says.

The spankings supposedly were not something that consumed the household, although Leon had a special place to sit—on the end of the front room couch—and Debbie would always sit across from him, in the rocking chair, when the spankings took place.

The others sat around, Velma often on the couch next to Lorraine, and Carolyn sat in another chair. The paddles, lath sticks about a foot-and-a-half long, sanded and rounded, were passed around and each took his turn swatting David a few times or many times, on his legs, his rear, his back, his arms—almost everywhere except the genitals and the kidney area. Leon said to always beware of the kidney area.

"Do yew have luv in y'r heart?" Leon would say to David.

"Yes," David would say.

"Then show it," Leon would say.

David would hug and kiss Leon.

But Leon did not think David was being honest. David had the devil in him. Leon could see it in the boy's face. He knew that was why David said he hated people, why David did all these things, why David did not show love when he hugged Leon the minister.

"Y'r not bein' true," Leon would say, and spank David again. Then it would be someone else's turn.

During the four months this went on, sometimes daily, sometimes only weekly, Leon realized the spankings were not having the effect the Bible predicted. David's case was unusual, Leon could see, in that it was not so much that the devil possessed David, but that David—when the devil was temporarily driven out by the spankings—would CALL the devil back within him. The "humblings" began. Leon and Debbie pushing David to the floor and ordering him up and spanking him when he failed to follow the orders. Leon was pleased with this, he could see the results almost instantly.

The devil-look would leave David's face when he was humbled.

On the morning of July 22, a hot summer Thursday in Yakima, David was given his morning swats. They apparently had no effect. By the afternoon, Leon could see the devil was still in David. It seemed that David even liked to be whipped, as Leon called it. "He wanted to be whipped an' the tail," Leon said.

Carolyn, the daughter, isn't sure now. But she thought David had gotten an extra-long spanking that afternoon. It seemed to last a half-hour. And it seemed David passed out afterwards.

David's mother remembers clearly, however, picking David up off the floor afterward. David seemed to be fighting. She turned around, swinging David by his arm and leg and then he fell. There was a tiny splotch of blood at his lips. Debra, Carolyn, Leon—they were amazed. They looked at little David Weilbacher, age 3, on the floor and they are all positive they saw a little boy raise his fists and growl. Within seconds, he had puffed up his chest twice, and stopped breathing.

Doctors are not part of the family's thinking. Only God is. Carolyn and Debbie picked up David and put him in the back bedroom of the house. There God would take care of him. No one cried, no one cared for David. His mother changed his underwear and left him, seemingly dead, maybe alive, on his bed. Two hours later, she pulled the covers up on him after bathing his body with a sponge. She did this every day for three days.

On the fourth, the family led by Leon, entered the room and said their final prayers over the boy. Leon lifted the body from the bed. "In the name of Jesus Christ, arise!" Leon said. Then the windows were painted, rags stuffed into cracks, the doors shut and taped. That Monday was the last time Leon and his family saw David Weilbacher and his demon spirit. But the Bible had been only half right.

The family kept a vigil to prevent the devil from returning to the old yellow house on S. 12th Street, one of the members sometimes staying up all night, praying while the others slept in all but one bedroom.

For two months, they prayed and awaited David's return, as Seth David, who would not have the black heart and the devil in his face.

On September 19, a person came to the door. It was not what they hoped. The person, Sgt. Robert Langdale, went to the back bedroom, to the door where deodorant had been sprayed to stop the smell, and Sgt. Robert Langdale busted through the door and got the shock of his life. With his gas mask on, looking under the sheet on a cot, Sgt. Robert Langdale saw something that was bloated, beaten, black, three feet long, and three-and-a-half years old.

A pathologist later would say there was no way in the world he could tell how David Weilbacher died. But he had a guess. He thought David Weilbacher had been beaten to death.

What was left of the boy was, two weeks later, lowered into a grave in a desolate, flatland part of the Tacoma Cemetery on the other side of town from where David Weilbacher had lived.

And what there is left of the boy today is a small stone marker over the grave.

The marker says:

"David Wellbacker."

The name, in stone, is misspelled. It is almost as if David Weilbacher never, ever really lived.

3. Unbidden Guest

Lawrence Madden

There was little doubt that the Thompson girl had become possessed. But by what? A demon, an evil spirit, some other unearthly entity? Surely not in Florida in the second half of the twentieth century! Yet, these were the facts (although names and other means of identification have been changed), and they were just terrifying and untidy enough to baffle and fascinate even a pair of tough, experienced newspapermen. Mr. Madden previously contributed "Can $300,000 Prove Man's Life Beyond Death?" to The Psychic Scene. He has once again taken up residence in Florida and is working on a novel set in the "Bermuda Triangle."

About the first of April 1974, I learned of the strange happenings in the Thompson household from news copy kindly lent to me by Arthur Thurston.

That spring I was in Miami visiting some not-very-close relatives and, intermittently, looking for work. It was natural that I should call Arty Thurston since he and I had started out as reporters together, and I hoped that, as city editor, he might find some work for me on his present paper. He could not, but he showed me some copy which had come across his desk regarding the Thompson house, the scene of disturbances which had lasted some two weeks. He was reluctant to print the story as a news item, not quite believing in the supernatural himself; but knowing that I was equally disinclined toward such beliefs, he suggested I might follow the story up, and he would run it as a curiosity feature in the Sunday supplement.

The reports themselves had been sent in by a Dr. John H.

Lesley. From these reports it appeared that the fourteen-year-old Thompson girl, Mary Elizabeth, had become "possessed" on March 17, and was thereafter the center of "telekinetic" activity. Accompanying the report were affidavits, not only from the doctor himself, but from the Reverend R. C. Archer (M.A., B.D.) minister of the local Baptist church; William Thompson, the stepfather of Mary Elizabeth, and his wife, Clyde, and her sister Mrs. Anna Bingham; Miss Margaret Shay, a certified teacher who had been with the public school system for twenty-one years; and Ralph Green (M.D., D.Sc.), a practicing psychiatrist; and his wife, Sarah, herself a qualified child therapist.

The Thompson house seemed an unlikely place for spooky doings; standing at 4343 N.W. Flagler Terrace, it was a two-story, frame affair, painted an unconvincing yellow with green trim; it had an air not so much of decay as of quiet discouragement, as if it were somewhat embarrassed by the gaudy red and blue stucco homes which the newly arrived Hispanics, mostly Cubans, had built around it since the Bay of Pigs debacle. William Thompson, age fifty-six, was a respectable sheet-metal worker who had risen to foreman of his shop. He had purchased the house with a mortgage in 1954.

There were four rooms on the ground floor, a living room, a large kitchen and dining room, and a small sewing room. Upstairs were two small bedrooms occupied by Mary Elizabeth and her half sister Kathy, age sixteen, and her aunt, Mrs. Bingham. The third room was used as an attic. There were bathrooms on both floors and a garage connected with the house and partially enclosed by a tool room. The small lawn was well kept and marked off by a foot-high rectangle of stones.

Mary Elizabeth was not William Thompson's natural daughter, but the daughter of his brother Henry. She had come from Orlando on January 12, 1974, because after her mother's death, Henry's family had fallen upon difficult times. The two older children in the family had been resettled with relatives, and the father had moved north with the two infants to settle in Virginia. Mary Elizabeth's life had been spent in or around Orlando, her father having worked the orange groves in that area. Despite the presence of brothers and sisters, Mary Elizabeth's upbringing was extremely quiet and lonely, the other children apparently considering her rather "strange." Her parents were elderly, and the only close companions Mary Elizabeth had were her pet Spaniel, Tab, and one friend, a nine-year-old girl, Susy.

On coming to live in her uncle's house, she shared the double bed at nights with Kathy. Kathy was extremely popular with her classmates at Miami Senior High School, being elected class president, and despite a slightly different coloring in her eyes, was considered something of "a beauty." Mary Elizabeth, I discovered, was short for her age and her still-lingering baby fat made her plumpish, with small hands and feet, curly hair boyishly cut, a round face with large large hazel eyes, crooked, badly cared-for teeth, and pale complexion. In temperament I found her to be gentle and easygoing, but I sensed from the first she had a strong, sulky will, one which easily flared into anger when she felt crossed.

Apart from the death of her mother, the separation from her father and family, the sudden presence of an older, attractive half sister, she had also experienced the relocation to a strange environment of blasting maringué music, sexually aggressive boys, and the isolation of living in a foreign language environment; the Thompsons were among the few remaining native American families in the neighborhood. All these changes had occurred from December 22, 1973, to January 12, 1974. There was also another, deeper emotional shock which only came to light during one of her later, possessed states.

It appears that her natural sister Maryanne, age sixteen, had been going steady with a young boy in her high school, Davy Masson. On the night of November 22, 1973, he had driven by Henry Thompson's house hoping to take Maryanne for a drive. Finding no one home but Mary Elizabeth, who was baby-sitting for the two younger children, he enticed her into his car, saying they would just "drive around the block." It was shortly before eight o'clock, and a light drizzle had set in. Masson parked the car in a secluded area a few blocks away from the house. He began telling her about the intimacies between himself and her sister, until she felt "stirred up." Exposing himself, and making other physical advances, he frightened her. But at the crucial moment, there was a flash of headlights from another car pulling up behind them. Masson hesitated, probably fearing it was the police who usually patrolled this "lovers' lane." Mary Elizabeth jumped from the car and ran home.

No medical examination of the girl was ever made, although the girl herself furiously maintained that "nothing had happened," a statement somewhat contradicted by what she revealed in her possessed state. She arrived home about ten o'clock, her hair and dress wet and disheveled. Distraught, she found that her parents had returned. She did not relate exactly what had happened to her, but went upstairs and locked herself in her bedroom. During the next four days, sensing the father's subdued rage, Mary Elizabeth did not tell her secret to anyone, not even her mother, who was sympathetic, but went about the house without saying a word, redeyed from sleeplessness and crying. From her appearance that night and her own defiant silence, her father could only surmise the worst. Doubtless Mary Elizabeth felt that this incident bore directly on her going to live with her Uncle William after her mother's death, since her father had reneged on an earlier promise that if her mother "went away," he should take her with him to Virginia so that she could "help" him look after the younger children.

Such was the emotional background of the case, as I found out from Dr. Lesley and members of the family. It was, of course, to Dr. Lesley that I first went to follow up on the reports which he had sent to Arty Thurston. I have selected from his statements, and those of other witnesses (which he has very generously agreed to let me quote), a "diary" of the main events which occurred before my own arrival on the scene.

On the evening of St. Patrick's Day, the first manifestations took place. Mary Elizabeth had gone to bed early, and when Kathy came in, she found her half sister crying as usual, her head buried in her pillow. When she asked what the matter was, she was not surprised at the answer. Mary Elizabeth reminded her that it was almost three months to the day since her mother had died. Kathy turned out the lights and got into bed. The two girls lay there without speaking.

Soon there was a hollow thumping in the room, as though a basketball was being slowly bounced; the sound moved down the stairs and into the living room. They went downstairs, but found nothing. When they came back to the bedroom, they saw an object moving under the bed clothes; it had the size and quickness of a mouse. Throwing the covers back, they discovered the object was continuing to move inside the mattress. Both girls watched the movement for several minutes, until it subsided. That night, they pulled the bed clothes off the bed and slept on the floor. There were no further disturbances. As with later occurrences, there were no manifestations when Mary Elizabeth was asleep, although they were intensified during her trance or "possessed" state.

Monday, March 18: Mary Elizabeth was allowed to stay home from school. That night, after she and Kathy had gone to bed, they again heard something thumping, although the sound was different from the previous night, and this time it came from the closet. The frightened girls opened the closet door and found the sounds were coming from a cardboard box filled with old clothes. They held the box between them—when it jumped nearly a foot in the air, striking Kathy in the face. Half angry, half laughing, she accused her sister of throwing the box at her. The box was then lying in the center of the room, with neither girl touching it. It jumped again.

Mary Elizabeth was standing a few feet away from the bedroom door, with her back to it, when Kathy saw the door swing open "nearly a foot." Mary Elizabeth turned, and both girls saw the door swing slowly closed. The girls then began screaming and ran downstairs to their parents' room. Sleepy and annoyed, their father came back to the bedroom with them. He searched the box and found nothing. He told both girls to go back to bed and that he would have "no more nonsense" from them. In the morning, he had apparently told their story to the rest of the family, who treated the matter as a joke.

Tuesday, March 19: Mary Elizabeth complained of feeling ill and was running a 100-degree temperature. She went up to bed after dinner, about eight o'clock. Kathy did not retire until shortly before midnight. She found her half sister sleeping; she undressed and turned out the light. About fifteen minutes later, she heard a gnashing of teeth and low masculine moans, so low that they sounded like the growling of an animal. "What's the matter?" she whispered, but there was no answer. Feeling Mary Elizabeth thrashing about, she got up and turned on the light.

Mary Elizabeth's face was a fiery red, her short hair stood on end as though electrified, her eyes, although staring wildly out of her head, seemed not to see the room about her, her hands were gripping the backboard of the bed so tightly that her fingernails left indentations in the wood. Most remarkable was her face, which "seemed all melted down, like an astronaut's when they take off." Kathy ran for her parents.

When they came into the room, they found Mary Elizabeth standing up. Helping her back into bed, they noticed that her whole body had begun to swell and was burning hot to the touch. Her facial muscles continued to writhe uncontrollably and she moaned, or rather "growled" with pain, gnashing her teeth. "She's having a fit," her stepfather announced to the family. Suddenly there was a snapping noise, "but loud as thunder," according to Clyde Thompson. Next, the alarm clock flew off the nighttable and struck William over the right eye, leaving a small trickle of blood. Thoroughly frightened, he left the room, saying he would never return.

There were three more snapping sounds, loud as gunshots, which seemed to be coming from behind the headboard of the bed. Mary Elizabeth's body had begun to lose its swelling. After a few minutes, her features returned to normal, and she fell asleep. Throughout the incident, her mouth had kept working as though she were trying to speak, but no sound had come from her lips but the strange, low moaning.

Gathering downstairs, the family discussed the incident among themselves and decided they would talk to no one about what had happened.

Wednesday, March 20: The next night, however, Mary Elizabeth had another seizure as she was about to get into bed, and William Thompson decided to call the family physician, Dr. Lesley. He arrived shortly before midnight, an hour after the fit had begun. All the symptoms were exactly as they had been the night before. Dr. Lesley registered her pulse, examined her throat, then muscle tone, which he found to be quite rigid and suffering from anesthesia. His preliminary diagnosis was that she was suffering from traumatic hysteria, due to some obscure emotional shock.

Hardly had he made his diagnosis, when a large seaman's trunk (twenty-seven inches long, twenty inches high, and seventeen inches deep, full of bed clothes, old silver and plates), which stood against the wall opposite the bed, began to rock slightly and then rose about two inches in the air, moved a distance of two feet, while still in the air, and then returned to its original position. This phenomenon was seen by both Dr. Lesley and by all members of the family.

Dr. Lesley, a strong man of sixty who plays tennis every day and is active in other sports, found he could move the chest only with difficulty. Finally, it was suggested that when the seizure passed, Kathy should return to the double bed so that she might keep watch over her half sister during the night. This suggestion was followed by violent, demanding knockings, loud enough to be heard all over the house and by the neighbors on each side. Investigating, Dr. Lesley found that the poundings came not from behind the headboard but from within it. This he ascertained by placing his palms on either side of the wood and feeling it vibrate without any other apparent movement. He invited the family to confirm his impression, which they did. Mary Elizabeth was by this time already relaxed and falling to sleep.

Kathy refused to return to the bed with Mary Elizabeth, so that the small storeroom had to be cleaned out and a cot and other temporary furniture installed.

Thursday, March 21: The Reverend R. C. Archer arrived at eight-thirty o'clock, as the Thompson family was cleaning up after dinner. Mary Elizabeth was by now suffering from general exhaustion and spent much of her time in bed, except for days when she was strong enough to attend school. The Reverend Mr. Archer stayed with the girl, talking to her and praying, until about ten o'clock, when the family gathered to pray for her recovery. Far from helping her, however, the prayers seemed to induce another "attack," as the family now called her fits of "possession." As the swelling, the hysterical paralysis, the low growling, and other symptoms resumed, Mr. Archer urged her to lie still. He raised the crucifix to pronounce the benediction, the bed clothes flew violently off the bed and settled in a heap over his head. Disintangling himself, with the help of the family, he managed to tuck Mary Elizabeth into bed again, but the blankets refused to stay on the bed.

The entire Thompson family and Mr. Archer sat on the edges of the bed to keep the bedding down. Their backs were to Mary Elizabeth when they heard her low moans meld themselves into a bass masculine voice, saying: "Child, you are mine. This is my begotten child." They turned to see the characteristic contortion her face assumed during these possessed states fading as she drifted into sleep.

During the next four days, minor manifestations continued, both upstairs and down, although Mary Elizabeth, seemingly exhausted from her ordeal, remained confined to her room. The Thompsons had tried to keep the affair a secret, but the continued comings and going of Dr. Lesley, and the strange sounds heard within the house, began to arouse local gossip. Their largely superstitious neighbors began gathering in front of the house and passersby declared they could hear the thumpings from the sidewalk. These knockings became much more frequent and, as before, they seemed to mark the apex of each "attack," after which Mary Elizabeth gradually returned to her normal state. During the possession state, however, the masculine voice was now always present and addressed the family, especially William Thompson, with obscene language and suggestions.

Dr. Lesley kept extensive notes on Mary Elizabeth's medical and psychological state during her illness. Regarding her entranced or "possessed" state, he wrote:

"During these attacks she usually endures considerable painful pressure in the back of her head, with an impairment of sight, hearing and touch. Her speech is limited, of course, to that of the possessing personality or entity. These symptoms are accompanied by a swelling of her body, especially hands, feet and the abdominal region. Convulsions. Anesthesia of various parts of the body occur, most commonly in her right arm, the affected area extending from her lower neck to her elbow. However, the anesthetized areas are not, as I had at first thought, general; the affected tissues are mottled, that is, are interspersed with normal tissue. I was able to satisfy myself on this point by performing certain routine tests: the insertion of needles into the flesh, etc.

"Attempts to apply drugs and other medicines brought on a fresh outburst of knockings and more severe convulsions; as the patient's psychological condition, already seemed to me precarious enough, I often refrained from the use of sedatives which her medical condition clearly required. Beyond sedation, I feel I can do no good in her present condition anyway; a cure, if there is to be one, must come either from God or be effected by the illness running its natural course."

Dr. Lesley was widely read and deeply interested in psychical research and psychosomatic medicine, but he had no experience with paranormal situations. Nevertheless, he believed that "in most cases of prima facie possession, the control of the 'spirit' is limited to a few days or a few weeks. One of the peculiar features of Mary Elizabeth's case," the doctor concluded, "is the intensity and the duration of it."

Tuesday, March 26: The Thompson family had by now become as used to paranormal phenomena about the house as, I suppose, anyone can. Dr. Lesley assured them that these hysterical seizures would run their course within another week. Hardly had they assumed a wait-and-see attitude when the manifestations took a sudden and more dangerous turn. On this night, the "demon voice" predicted that the Thompson house would burn down!

Wednesday, March 27: At dinner, the Thompson family nervously watched Mary Elizabeth, although she seemed quite normal. Suddenly, a "ball of fire, about the size of a golf ball," was seen to materialize in midair and fall into the clothes hamper in the bathroom (which was situated eight feet from the dining room table). After much commotion, the smoldering linen was doused out with water. Mary Elizabeth had been sitting with her back to the hamper.

Thursday, March 28: Fifteen balls of fire (eight on the bottom floor, seven on the top floor) were seen to fall during the course of the day. The inflammable substance could not be identified, as its ashes were indistinguishable from that which had been set on fire.

Friday, March 29: The "spirit" arson continued. About five o'clock in the afternoon, there was another pounding in the house, this time in the living room. Again, it sounded like a gun shot. When it occurred, Kathy was cleaning the kitchen; Clyde and Mary Elizabeth were out back, washing clothes. Both girls had arrived home from school shortly after three o'clock. For about an hour Mary Elizabeth had helped Kathy in the kitchen, until her stepmother called her to help with the washing (about four-thirty o'clock). She had not been out of the sight of one of them since arriving home.

Having become accustomed to such noises, all the women were slow to investigate. When they got to the living room, they found the china cabinet had "blown up" and the wood was ablaze. A great deal of smoke had filled the living room and they were unable to put it out. Forced to call the local fire department, they found the firemen extremely suspicious of the blaze. Upon being told the story behind the repeated arsons, the firemen reacted with anger and alarm, warning Cylde Thompson that "action" would be taken if there were any recurrence of the incident.

The fires and other manifestations continued on March 30 and 31. Mary Elizabeth's possessed states continued throughout the last week in March, but there was no longer any direct correlation between the manifestations and her seizures. Nevertheless, William Thompson, who admitted to me that he had never liked the girl, arranged with Dr. Lesley to have Mary Elizabeth stay at the home of his friends, Drs. Ralph and Sarah Green.

It was during this period, April 4 and 5, that I first met Dr. Lesley, the Reverend Mr. Archer, and the Thompson family. Because of her absence and the reluctance of all concerned to have me do so, I did not meet Mary Elizabeth herself until the week before Easter, on April 7. Again for a four-day period, April 1 to 4, the manifestations ceased.

Friday, April 5: The manifestations resumed, knockings and fires, although only in a mild way. Despite the evident danger to their house, Ralph and Sarah Green continued their psychiatric examinations and held to the belief that all of the phenomena were caused by the girl herself. The main difficulty which Dr. Green experienced was his inability to build any association in Mary Elizabeth's mind between her normal and her "possessed" states. The girl obstinately refused any recollection or responsibility concerning the "spirit's" actions.

Saturday, April 6: While talking to Mary Elizabeth in his office, a wash basin filled with water, which sat on a sink about two feet from the girl, suddenly flew into the air, splashing the water in his face. While he told his wife about the incident, he concluded that Mary Elizabeth had performed the act herself although she was hypnotized and that she was "just extraordinarily quick." Although she was not present at the time, this was a judgment with which Sarah did not entirely agree.

Sunday, April 7: This evening, Mary Elizabeth became entranced. In the company of Dr. Lesley and Mr. Archer, I was invited to the Green household. I was astonished by the facial changes which took place in Mary Elizabeth. Her normally round, pudgy face seemed to elongate, even her chin seemed to draw itself into a sharp V, as did her mouth and nose, each making smaller Vs in their turn and, like the widow's peak of her hair, all pointing downward—except for her bushy and brown eyebrows which, by some muscular contortion, pointed in a V-shape upward until they nearly touched her hairline. Other symptoms of her possession were as I have already described.

We watched the girl in her agony (I don't know what else to call it) for slightly more than half an hour, during which time Mr. Archer left the room to call one of his parishioners who had been hospitalized. Dr. Lesley, Ralph and Sarah Green, and I continued to observe the girl. Her hands were quite visible and tightly clenched on the bedboard when we heard the scratching, as though a knife were being used to carve cement. Looking up, we saw a cross, forming itself upside down. Fascinated, we watched letters begin to form themselves underneath. At first they made no sense to any of us, until Dr. Lesley recognized them as Latin words spelled backwards, and translated them: "I am the Elder Son." The lettering and cross appeared some three feet above Mary Elizabeth's bed and, since we were standing at the foot of the bed, more than six feet from any others present in the room.

There was an explosion in the living room, and Sarah and I rushed in, leaving Drs. Lesley and Green to watch Mary Elizabeth. We found Mr. Archer still holding the phone, although somewhat dazed and bruised and holding his head with one hand; a large piece of plaster was broken at his feet. There was a large hole in the opposite corner of the ceiling, twenty-two feet away. It was decided that Mary Elizabeth should be returned to the Thompsons the following day.

Monday, April 8: I had my first chance to talk with Mary Elizabeth alone. I found her quite relaxed and at ease in her answers, confirming all about her that I had heard from her elders, but disclaiming any knowledge of what took place during her possessed states. When I questioned her about any "private communications" she might have had with her "spirit," she became ill at ease, suspicious, almost truculent in her replies.

I had recorded our conversation and was playing back the tape in the living room, making notes, when Mary Elizabeth came in and asked if she might listen to herself. I said yes, and continued listening to the tape, but all the while keeping my eyes on Mary Elizabeth. She did not sit down but stood across the room with her back to a bureau. After a few minutes, I saw a glass ashtray rise about a foot in the air, saw it not only with my naked eye but in the mirror which topped the bureau. It poised in the air for a moment, then flew across the room, narrowly missing my head as it fell sideways. Quite astonished, I stared at Mary Elizabeth, not sure whether I ought to rebuke her for such tricks or not. Her expression did not change. She left the room without a word.

Tuesday, April 9: Miss Margaret Shay, Mary Elizabeth's homeroom teacher, reported a manifestation in the schoolroom. It was during the study hours, and Miss Shay noticed that Mary Elizabeth was becoming increasingly nervous as she struggled with a math problem. She called the child to her desk, and while she was concentrating on helping Mary Elizabeth with the problem, Miss Shay felt the desk rise. It rose about an inch in the air, and she could feel the vibrations within the wood in her hands. Mary Elizabeth, at this moment, had stepped back and was standing about two feet away, her hands behind her back. None of the children appeared to have noticed the incident. After the desk settled gently back to the floor, Miss Shay went over it thoroughly, looking for some apparatus. She felt some trick had been played upon her, but the desk appeared perfectly normal.

Wednesday, April 10: Children do not usually make reliable witnesses because they are too suggestible. However, in the case of this day's manifestation, some credence might be given to their story. Mary Elizabeth fell into trance at school, attended by convulsions, and while Miss Shay's attention was engaged, the children claim that a piece of chalk rose in the air and quickly scrawled several obscenities regarding the teacher upon the blackboard. This was seen to happen by about twenty of the thirty students in the class. The "demon voice" did not appear during the trance, but the obscenities were quite in keeping with its usual utterances. Miss Shay was unfamiliar with the handwriting.

If I had not witnessed the lettering on the wall at the Green dwelling myself, I would be inclined to dismiss this whole incident as a childish prank.

Thursday, April 11: Mary Elizabeth accompanied her aunt, Mrs. Bingham, to the "social" which was held at Mr. Archer's church. While they sat alone in the front pew, talking with him about the recent events and the possibility of a Baptist minister performing an exorcism, one of the mysterious balls of fire was seen to fall on the altar cloth. Before Mr. Archer could find the means to put out the fire, the cloth was badly burned.

Friday, April 12: Good Friday. I don't know whether this date is significant—probably not. Mary Elizabeth went through unusually violent convulsions tonight, suffering one of the worst spells I have seen the girl endure. The "voice" was especially virulent, making extreme threats ("prophecies," it calls them) against the Reverend Mr. Archer and his church. Most startling was the prediction that his church would burn down tonight!

According to her mother, Mary Elizabeth kept the family up unusually late, not dropping off to sleep until well after midnight. Whether the girl remained in the house or awoke and left is not certain. What is certain is that at 3:10 A.M. the neighborhood was awakened by the sound of fire engines racing to the Baptist church, five blocks away. The church, an old wooden structure went up quickly in the blaze. The firemen, arriving late, termed the origin of the fire "suspicious," but gave no details as to why they thought so.

Saturday, April 13: Mary Elizabeth was much quieter today. There were only two significant phenomena. In the afternoon, Clyde and Mrs. Bingham were helping Mary Elizabeth straighten up her room. A laundry bag, which hung on the inside of the closet door, suddenly began to jump about, "as though a dog or something was caught in there." When I talked to Mrs. Bingham about the incident, I asked, "Could it have been a large mouse?" (The "mouse" manifestations have continued throughout this case.) "It could've been, but it wasn't." "What did you do?" I asked. "I went and opened it. The bag was still jumpin' around in my hand when I took it down." "That was very brave of you," I replied. "What did you find?" The old woman looked away from me, sadly. "I found just what I thought I'd find. Nothin.' Just nothin'."

The second phenomenon occurred during dinner. The front door, which is twenty-four feet from the table, opened suddenly and slammed closed, as though somebody were leaving angrily.

After dinner the Reverend Mr. Archer came over, took William Thompson and his wife aside, and confided to them the decision which the deacons of the church had taken. Over his objections, they were bringing Mary Elizabeth before the juvenile court on a charge of arson.

Sunday, April 14: Mary Elizabeth was quiet. There were no manifestations today, and it appears that at this time they ceased altogether. The coincidence of this fact with Easter Sunday may be significant, but I am inclined to discount it. The chain of events with four-day intervals, lasted exactly a lunar month, twenty-eight days, as Dr. Lesley had thought, and they had probably just run their natural course.

The feature article which I wrote proved to be too long and, of course, too late. Mary Elizabeth was taken before the juvenile court, and although no sentence was passed because it was her first offense, and because of the unusual circumstances surrounding the case, she was remanded to Jackson Memorial Hospital for extensive psychiatric treatment. Arty Thurston saw the story as "just another arson case." But he reached into his own pocket and gave me $200, because "of all the work you've put in." I had the feeling, however, that the money, at least in part, was to placate his skepticism which, like my own, had been badly shaken by the strange events in the Thompson house.

In April of 1977, I again found myself in Miami at Easter time, and my thoughts very naturally turned to Mary Elizabeth. I wondered what had become of her and thought there might be a good story in the aftermath. I drove out to the Thompson place. William Thompson was not happy to see me; he did not know where Mary Elizabeth was, did not want to know where she was, and all but told me to go mind my own business. But I wanted to know where she was, still thinking there might be a story in it for me.

There wasn't. It appears that Mary Elizabeth had never gone to the hospital for treatment; instead, she had run away. She had not changed her name and was working as a clerk in a Jacksonville department store. Because of her employment, it took only about two weeks to find her—if anyone, including the police, had been interested in finding her.

When I entered the small house on Lexington Avenue (little more than a shack really, stuck away behind a larger house), I scarcely recognized her. She looked much older than her eighteen years, fatter than I remembered, more frowsy, and had dyed her hair blond, which didn't help a bit. I also didn't like the man she was living with. She didn't seem too happy with him, either, and toward me she was sullen and recalcitrant. She said she didn't remember the events of three years before, that she had told everything she knew at the time. Her man took her aside and talked with her for a few minutes, and then came back to me. He said Mary Elizabeth would be willing to talk to me if I would give them $500. I made up my mind that I liked him even less than I thought I did, and as for Mary Elizabeth, I knew her to be quite inventive enough to say anything. There was no sense in pursuing the situation, and I came away empty-handed.

With regard to the events themselves: Unquestionably, some of them were faked. Some of the manifestations, particularly the fire phenomena, were within the ingenuity of any bright, nimble teen-ager; just as certainly, some of the manifestations seem to defy any normal explanation. The only conclusion, it seems to me, is that Mary Elizabeth helped along the genuine manifestations in any way she could.

But were the phenomena real, or were they the product of mistakes and hallucination? Naturally, in answering this question, I remove my own testimony as evidence, since in only one instance did I have corroborating witnesses. One person surely could be deceived and repeatedly deceived. However, it is unlikely that so many responsible people, over the period of a month, could repeatedly be deceived about what they saw as a group. Also, with minor variations, their descriptions are consistent with one another. We must conclude that the phenomena were real, at least in the sense that *something* took place.

In cases as bizarre as this one, we must always consider the possibility of collusion. However, some of the witnesses, such as William Thompson, were openly hostile to Mary Elizabeth; others, such as the Reverend Mr. Archer, were the victims of the manifestations; others, such as Drs. Lesley and the Greens, apart from the objectivity they brought to bear on the case, would scarcely have risked their professional reputations and livelihoods for a casual prank. No, fraud does not seem a very probable explanation.

Given the age of the Thompson house, it is possible that shifts in the earth, underground water, or some other natural causes, might account for some of the phenomena, such as the opening and closing of doors, noises, and the movement of other objects. But the variety of the manifestations and the fact that they took place in different locales rules this possibility out as a general explanation.

Even when all these explanations are taken together, to explain this or that piece of evidence, there seems to remain a hard core of phenomena which is real and which cannot be explained by normal means. We may decide that Mary Elizabeth was the agency of a poltergeist or possessed by a demon or an unconscious medium or the victim of hysteria and a split personality. In truth, she was probably a bit of all these, but none of these explanations lead us to the central core of the problem, which is, simply, how is it possible for thoughts, or strong emotions, to translate themselves into physical actions, except by the normal means? Psychological explanations may explain "why" certain phenomena occurred, but they cannot explain "how" they occurred.

As a reporter, I cannot pretend to answer that question; from only the facts of this case, I don't think the question can be answered. We must be satisfied by knowing that such phenomena can occur, although rarely. For myself, it is sufficient to know they *do* occur; that alone has been enough to change my whole outlook on life, both of the world I live in and of my own life.

4. Satan in Daly City

Leland Joachim

*The setting is totally contemporary: Daly City, the San Fran-
cisco suburb, just a few years ago. The events are as traditional as they are specific: a diabolical force appears to seek
control of an infant, and is driven out by exorcisms performed by a priest. While the identity of the Daly City
family has remained guarded by church authorities, the exorcist, the Reverend Karl Patzelt, is well known as a member
of the Jesuit order and has provided details of the case; he
concluded that the family has "lived happily ever after." Le-
land Joachim a member of the editorial staff of the* San Jose
Mercury, *has published magazine articles on psychic subjects.*

When the Devil terrorized a family in Daly City, California,
for several months in 1972 and 1973, was he trying to gain
possession of a two-year-old boy? If so, he never succeeded,
though the "thousand tricks" he employed finally drove the
couple to seek the help of an exorcist.

Indeed, the infant may have been possessed by quite another sort of spirit, to judge by one of the incidents that happened while the house was in the grip of the strange
tormentor. Again and again, some mysterious occurrence—all
the more terrifying because it was happening to the boy—
would be directed against him, though he never was harmed.

The demonic phenomena began when the cries of the two-
year-old awoke the young parents one night. They rushed
into his room to find that some force had picked up a rocking
chair and placed it in the crib, squarely on the squirming
infant. They quickly removed the chair. Finding their son
unhurt, they soon had him comforted enough so they could

return to bed. They needed their sleep, having been allowed only two hours of peace each night, from 4 to 6 A.M. for several months.

The family—their names have never been divulged—first came under the strange attacks during a ten-week period in the spring of 1972. Shoes were thrown, windows broken, and towels set afire. Some unseen presence rained blows on them.

The mysterious incidents stopped, then started again in May of 1973. It was not until fall that the couple contacted the Reverend Karl Patzelt, S.J., pastor of Our Lady of Fatima Church in San Francisco. Father Patzelt, then 57, was a Jesuit and a priest of the Russian Rite of the Catholic Church. Father Patzelt later described what he found when he came to the home. He said one or the other of the parents would scream in pain, crying out that they were being choked by a strong, invisible force. Bruises were left on their throats. Father Patzelt said a doctor saw the bruises and said they were genuine.

Objects as big as chairs were moved about. Father Patzelt said the parents often were buffeted by the unseen presence, and the woman once was knocked unconscious. The two-year-old grasped a small statue of the Virgin Mary and toddled over to his mother. He held the statue aloft and shouted: "Devil out! Devil out!" The statue may have protected him. At any rate, he suffered no harm, and his mother soon recovered consciousness.

Poltergeists might be suspected, or if you prefer, the paranormal abilities ascribed to adolescents who cause objects to go flying across rooms or furniture to be mysteriously moved around. But there were no adolescents in the house, only the two-year-old, and a menace more ancient than mankind.

Father Patzelt had never attempted an exorcism, but he knew the ritual. He visited the house for twenty-nine consecutive days. Assisted by twenty lay church members, he prayed, swung incense in every room, and recited the rites of exorcism dating back to 1614, during the time of Pope Paul V: "Strike terror, Lord, into the beast now laying waste your vineyard. Fill your servants with courage to fight manfully against that reprobate dragon, lest he despise those who put their trust in you . . ."

The Reverend Miles O'Brien Riley, director of the San Francisco Archdiocese Communications Center, said, "The case is a reminder the Devil is alive and well—and so is good. Evil is real, powerful and present—and so is goodness."

Father Patzelt and his helpers labored on. "I command you, unclean spirit, whoever you are, along with all your minions now attacking this servant of God . . . that you tell me by some sign your name, and the day and hour of your departure. I command you, moreover, to obey me to the letter, I who am a minister of God despite my unworthiness; nor shall you be emboldened to harm in any way this creature of God, or the bystanders, or any of their possessions."

The case was first described in Catholic publications. When reporters learned of the incident, the archdiocese confirmed that an exorcism had taken place, but refused to divulge the name of the family or their address, saying it would be "immoral and unfair" to them.

Father Patzelt described the family as "very average." The husband worked for United Airlines at San Francisco International Airport. Why they had been selected for attacks from the Devil, the priest couldn't say. A decisive change happened as he recited the last of the rites. "I cast you out, unclean spirits, along with every Satanic power of the enemy, every specter from Hell and all your fell companions." A great wave of searing heat rushed into the room. Father Patzelt gasped. Sweat beaded on his forehead. Was the Devil about to conjure up some horror that would make his other tricks pale by comparison?

"Hearken therefore, and tremble in fear, Satan, you enemy of the faith, you foe of the human race, you begetter of death, you robber of life, you corruptor of justice, you root of all evil and vice, seducer of men, betrayor of nations, instigator of envy, font of avarice, formenter of discord, author of pain and sorrow."

The heat was stifling, unbearable.

"Why then, do you stand and resist, knowing as you must that Christ, the Lord, brings your plans to nothing? . . . Begone, then, in the name of the Father and of the Son and of the Holy Spirit."

Suddenly there was peace. Father Patzelt said later: "Nothing has happened since."

The triumphant priest flew to New York to appear on the "Tomorrow" television show. He showed photographs taken in the Daly City home. One showed a sandwich prepared by the mother, with a large bite missing. It had been taken when she turned her back to prepare something else. Another showed a scorched bathroom wall where a towel caught fire, another an upended footrest which spontaneously erupted into flame along with a piece of cloth, another a burned and partially melted wastebasket which caught fire during the priest's second visit to the home. All were attributed to the Devil's "tricks."

The exorcist told his nationwide audience the devil is real and many mental cases may actually be the fault of demonic possession: "It is important to bring clarity to these things, so that persons affected know there is a solution. There are more persons possessed than we think, and many of those in mental institutions do not belong there. They belong in the hands of priests."

A debate arose among priests, with here and there a psychiatrist muttering, "Mumbo jumbo!" Father Patzelt closed the door on further inquiries, stating: "In what I feel are the best interests of all concerned, I shall not consent to any more interviews or answer questions other than those posed by proper church authorities." He added: "A serious and intensive investigation was carried out before the question of diabolical intervention was even considered. The investigation included reports from two psychiatrists who lived with the family ten days, as well as medical examinations of those involved. Only after mature reflection and serious consideration and examination of the situation was the possibility of performing exorcism considered."

His four-page statement said that while Father Patzelt was at the home "the Devil revealed himself each time during the service by knocking both husband and wife down, often to the point of unconsciousness, choking them, twisting their arms behind their backs. Only the touch of the relic of the Holy Cross brought immediate relief, or brought them back to consciousness."

Both church leaders and psychiatrists expressed fears that more publicity would lead the mentally unstable to believe they were possessed by demons. Archbishop Joseph T. McGucken, who approved the exorcism, was reported to have misgivings about the incident. The church seemed afraid of being overrun with more potential exorcisms than it could possibly investigate.

But others expressed their views on the significance of the exorcism. Dr. William Bellamy, a San Francisco psychoanalyst, said that the power of suggestion could affect many immature and insecure people who already feel the world is alien and populated by influences evil to them. He said his training indicated that persons who believe they are possessed by the Devil "usually" are suffering "delusion and schizophrenia." (Well, Dr. Bellamy left himself some room with that "usually.") He also said he has seen "literally thousands" of deluded persons who thought they were possessed.

How many witches, burned in Salem, would have wound up on the psychiatrists' couches if they lived in our times?

A Catholic theologian, the Reverend Peter Riga of St. Mary's College, scolded church authorities for permitting the exorcism. He told reporters "This nonsense is raising havoc with the people. I have had six people come to me within the past week saying they think they are obsessed." Father Riga was blunt in his criticism of the archbishop. He called approval of the ritual "a public scandal," and called it "unfortunate that the Catholic Church in San Francisco in its Madison Avenue putsch" is "leading many people to really believe in the medieval superstition of possession-obsession, Devil wizardry."

Father Riga said that while the archbishop may have acted in accordance with canon law, the ritual dates from a period when "Christianity was enmeshed with paganism." He said its use today was a setback for theologians "who have been trying to demythologize" church teachings.

The Reverend Theodore Mackin of the University of Santa Clara confessed to "some slight doubt" about the existence of devils, but said he believed "there are such creatures as angels, purely spiritual creatures. I find it believable that some may be sort of locked in hatred of God and all other creatures. I believe there are devils." Whether there is a "head Devil" is another question, Father Mackin said, and there is a lot of "anthropomorphism in that." Men "sort of create a social arrangement for the Devil, patterned after the human model of a head man."

Father Mackin agreed with Dr. Bellamy that persons who think they are possessed usually suffer from delusions; he said, "There seemed to be a great number of people who would like to explain away the pains of their soul (unhappiness) by finding a scapegoat, by saying 'The Devil made me do it.'" Father Mackin also said: "Add to this the morbid fascination many people have, and you have a kind of religious necrophilia. There will be people thinking diabolic possession all over the landscape."

He said further his "real worry is that it muddles up the accurate image of God, of Christ, of what goodness really is. The center stage is occupied with things like possession, where it should be occupied with things like compassion, concern for the poor, the political prisoner. Exorcism is a great red herring."

For Bernard Cooke, theology professor at the University of Windsor, there definitely are "personal sources of evil." Cooke said, however: "I don't think there's anything that absolutely necessitates the existence of devils in the sources of Catholic teaching. I personally don't see absolutely convincing evidence one way or the other. I'm sure there is a personal dimension of evil, but I'm not so sure you have to go beyond the human to see it."

Cooke, a former Jesuit, raised the question of psychic energy and said even if no Devil is present, the rites of exorcism can be very beneficial, by "ridding people of whatever influence is causing their problem." He said, "If it heals the situation, fine, it's better to do that."

While theologians speculate, Father Patzelt's belief in possession and obsession (in which the place, rather than the person, is occupied) has remained unshaken. He still is at Our Lady of Fatima, where he answers the telephone himself.

Asked what has happened to the bedeviled family since the exorcism, Father Patzelt replied, "They lived happily ever after," but declined to answer questions about their whereabouts.

Father Patzelt was asked whether he had performed other exorcisms since. "Plenty," he replied.

How many?

"I've lost count."

All his exorcisms, he explained, have been in the San Francisco Bay Area. "When someone in Oregon or Colorado contacts me, I refer them to priests in their area. There are priests all over who do this. I'm not a unique fellow. There are priests all over who can do it. It's their parish duty. When people are in trouble, they should help them."

5. The Washington-St. Louis Case
Michael Ballantine

During the current decade, interest in possession and exor-
cism was strongly stimulated by the novel and motion picture
The Exorcist. *Written by William Blatty, this fictional ac-*
count had its origin in a case of demon possession of a boy
that had occurred near Washington, D.C., at a time when
Blatty was a student at Georgetown University, in the na-
tion's capital. Mr. Ballantine, who has made a special study
of the history of psychical phenomena in the New England
region, has pieced together the hidden elements of the real
case behind the Blatty novel; as presented here, they are the
closest an outsider has yet come to narrating the facts behind
the dramatic motion picture, which was followed by a sequel,
The Heretic: Exorcist II.

If we can give the boy a name, Douglass Deen is as a good
as any. It was this name that was first published in the newspaper accounts, back in 1949, when young Deen's case originally occurred. And, although this was not his real name, we
might as well use it in this behind-the-scenes report. The
parents of young Deen did not actually live in Washington,
but in a suburb, Mount Rainier. And although the whole
family was eventually converted to Roman Catholicism, they
had belonged to the Lutheran Church. Douglass first became
the center of weird phenomena when he was thirteen years
old; the boy's frightening behavior lasted beyond his four-
teenth birthday.

The Deens had been close to an aunt of the child, a
woman who engaged in spiritistic practices, such as receiving
messages from departed spirits on a Ouija board. Douglass
continued to experiment with such a talking board after his

aunt's death, apparently in an effort to contact her discarnate spirit. The Reverend John J. Nicola, in his book *Diabolical Possession and Exorcism* (Rockford, Ill., 1974) published a thinly disguised account of the Deen case in which he speaks of the boy as "an only child," living "with his parents and his grandparents." His father was a truck driver. Father Nicola, who acted as a technical assistant during the filming of *The Exorcist*, describes Douglass as "not in any way outstanding," as "mildly extroverted, casually respectful of his elders and superiors, and moderately enthusiastic in the practice of his Lutheran religion."

In November 1948, Douglass reported hearing strange noises in his bedroom. At first, the parents ignored these remarks, discounting them as a means of getting attention. But when the boy persisted, his mother came to find out what was happening and she, too, heard scratching sounds. The parents decided that rats or mice might be causing the noises. An exterminator was brought to find out whether rodents were nesting under the floor boards in the boy's room or in the basement under it. Nothing was found, but the sounds persisted.

The idea that Douglass might be demon-possessed had not yet occurred to the Deen family. The scratching noises continued into early 1949. They were supplemented by other unexplained phenomena of the poltergeist type; in the history of psychic research, such phenomena are often associated with prepuberty adolescence. Douglass was relatively small for his age, weighed about ninety pounds and, Father Nicola has noted, "relatively immature." The poltergeist phenomena began to include flying dishes, squeaking footsteps in the hall, furniture moving back and forth across the floors of various rooms.

D. R. Linson reported on the case in *Fate* magazine (April 1951) that "from a bowl on top of the refrigerator, fruit leaped forth, either to hurl itself against the wall or to smash in a mess upon the floor. A picture darted abruptly from a wall. For a brief moment the picture quivered in the air, then with the rapidity that marked its departure from the wall, it snapped back into place."

Night after night the bed in which Douglas slept trembled violently. By then, the whole family was constantly aware of these disturbing phenomena. But when Mrs. Deen visited neighbors, she encountered disbelief and ridicule. Neighbors even offered to have the Deen boy sleep in their house. But the boy seemed to bring the phenomena with him. The neighbors were quickly convinced, once they, too, had witnessed the inexplicable events, that something unusual and terror-inducing was taking place in the boy's presence.

The Deen family became more and more distraught, as the phenomena mounted and grew increasingly intolerable. They were puzzled by the often quite meaningless nature of the phenomena. Once, for example, the boy's clothes, which he had thrown on a chair before going to bed, were found the next morning on top of the kitchen refrigerator. At this point, Father Nicola states, "a certain uneasiness began to become conspicuous around the house, although at this stage, everyone was convinced that someone in the house was sleepwalking or playing tricks on the rest of the family." Quite naturally, suspicion centered on young Douglass. Father Nicola also reports:

"A climax was reached one Sunday afternoon when relatives from out of town were visiting. All were seated around the living room talking, when suddenly the large easy chair on which the boy was seated seemed to levitate slightly and flip over backwards, the boy somersaulting onto the floor in the process. Immediately, his father and uncle righted the chair and, in turn, seated themselves in the chair, and attempted without success intentionally to induce the same reaction. While all were discussing the strange tumble, someone called attention to a vase on a small table. All stared spellbound as the vase rose slowly and hung suspended in the air. Then suddenly it hurtled across the room at an incredible speed and smashed against the wall, the sharp fragments scattering about the room. Fortunately no one was hurt."

One day, while Douglass was in school, the desk-and-seat combination on which he sat began to slither across the school room. The incident not only threw the whole class into an uproar and greatly upset the boy's teacher, it was also the subject of much gossip and speculation throughout the whole school for several days. Young Deen had become so notorious that, from then on, he had to be tutored at home. A medical examination of Douglass showed him to be normal, except for some "nervous tension," which might well be the result of the phenomena he had experienced. However, by then he did show symptoms of withdrawal and depression. He was subject to nightmares and often screamed in his sleep. Psychiatric examinations and psychological tests never-theless showed him as quite normal.

At this point, the notion that Douglass was engaged in some sort of prank was still being considered likely by the consulted physicians and psychiatrists. The family did not know what to make of it all. The three adults were them-selves, showing signs of strain. Grandmother, father, and mother once rushed into the boy's room when they heard him shout in his sleep. As they watched in awe and disbelief, a dresser in the boy's room slid across the floor and stopped only when it reached the door. The dresser drawers then opened and closed, one by one. These phenomena occurred, Father Nicola notes, "though no one was within ten feet of the dresser." He adds: "Similar levitation and telekinesis of articles was witnessed by friends and neighbors, but the psy-chiatrist remained convinced that these reports were halluci-natory."

Not knowing where else to turn, the boy's parents went to the local Luthern minister, the Reverend Mr. Winston. The minister's first reaction, on hearing their story, was also one of disbelief. But when they insisted, Winston agreed to have young Douglass stay with him at the parsonage for a few days. The minister felt sure that, once the boy was away from home, the phenomena would cease with the whole story exposed as a hoax.

To make sure that Douglass would not be able to devise any tricks, Mr. Winston arranged for the boy to share a room with him. On February 17, 1949, Douglass stayed in the par-sonage from 9:20 P.M. to 9:20 A.M. of the following day. By ten o'clock at night, the minister and boy retired, using twin beds. All was uneventful for about ten minutes. Then, accord-ing to a report Mr. Winston delivered the following August 9 at the Society for Parapsychology in Washington, there were "tremendous vibrations" from the boy's bed, which coincided with "scraping and scratching noises from the wall."

At this point, the minister jumped out of bed and turned on the light. He saw that the vibration of the bed continued. Watching Douglass carefully, he sought to trace the move-ment and sounds to some physical action on the boy's part. He did not see the youngster move and later commented: "While I seemed to sense in my heart that he was not creating these effects, and while I had seen similar activities occur at the boy's home and in the presence of his parents, I just had to make sure."

The next phenomenon occurred when the Reverend Mr. Winston asked Douglass to get out of bed and sit in a big armchair. The youngster pulled up his feet, so that his knees were under his chin, and the minister wrapped him into a blanket. Douglass' hands and arms were clutched around his raised-up legs. According to the Linson magazine account, this is what happened next: "Before the startled eyes of the minister, the chair began to move! It moved three inches until it reached the wall and could go no farther in that direction. During this time the pastor stood in front of the chair. Amazed, he watched intently. The lights were on, and in the brightly lighted room the phenomena that subsequently occurred seemed incredible."

What followed was this: The big, heavy armchair continued to move across the room, with Douglass sitting right in it; once the chair reached the wall, coming to a stop, it began to tip and finally tilted completely over. Douglass anticipated the final movement, telling the Reverend Winston, "It's going over with me, Pastor." At that point, the chair fell over completely, and the boy was thrown to the floor. Next, Mr. Winston sat in the chair himself, but there was no motion. He could tip the chair only by pushing with his feet and turning violently from side to side.

As the motions of the bed had made it impossible for Douglass to sleep, the Lutheran minister constructed an emergency bed directly on the floor. He put down a mattress, a pillow, covered the boy with a blanket, and the youngster quickly fell asleep. The clergyman remained awake and kept the lights burning. While he watched the boy, the whole sleeping unit began to slide across the floor. Douglass woke up when his head hit part of the bed, at the other end of the room. When Mr. Winston rearranged the emergency bed all over again, the combination started to move in a circle around the room, with the mattress sliding under the bed. As he recalled later, the minister observed that the boy's hands remained inside the bedding, his body rigid enough to make it impossible for him to manipulate the movement of the emergency bed in any way; even the blankets were not twisted by the curious movement.

The Reverend Mr. Winston told his Washington listeners later that year, "What convinced me was that the whole thing moved as a unit." Winston was, by that time, certain that something supernatural was happening to Douglass Deen, but felt powerless to provide guidance to the family or offer any "cure" for whatever was happening to the young boy.

Douglass was taken to Georgetown University, a Jesuit institution, for medical and psychiatric care. Drugs and intravenous glucose feeding were used to stop the child's emotional and physical debilitation. By that time, the youngster's body had become directly affected, with seizures that resembled *grand mal* epileptic attacks. Father Nicola's account notes that family and doctors feared that malnutrition would completely undermine Douglass' already precarious health. He writes that "at this time also the signs of multiple personality began to surface. At times the boy was almost his pleasant normal self; at other times his facial features would be contorted, and he would speak in a deep, gravelly, raucous voice, using the most obscene and degrading language."

The Reverend Mr. Winston, one night at dinner, mentioned the case to a friend who was a Roman Catholic priest. They agreed that the Catholic exorcism ritual might be helpful in this case and obtained the agreement of the distraught parents that this road be tried. But when an exorcism was attempted at their home, news of it spread quickly, and the participants agreed that it might be wise to take young Douglass to another city, so that an exorcism could be done in complete secrecy. One night, the boy's parents observed welts on his leg that appeared to spell out the words, "GO ST LOUIS." This encouraged them to agree that Douglass be taken to St. Louis for his exorcism. He had an uncle in that city, who reported the case to an acquaintance, Father Raymond Bishop, S.J., who in turn approached the local Catholic diocese.

The decision to go ahead with the exorcism in St. Louis was made by Archbishop Ritter. This step has been criticized by one authority, Dr. Henry Ansgar Kelly. In his book *The Devil, Demonology and Witchcraft* (New York, 1974), he refers to the archbishop's decision as having been made "without further investigation." According to this account, the priest who was asked to undertake the exorcism, Father William S. Bowdern, S.J., received his orders "like a bolt out of the blue," but, after studying the rite outlined in the *Rituale Romanum*—the sixteenth-century guide—sought to proceed immediately.

The exorcism period lasted for thirty-five days and was an excruciating experience for all who participated in it. As Dr. Kelly sees it, "the action was clearly premature," as "it would have been proper first of all to consider the possibility" that the phenomena "were not of an evil, and, specifically, diabolical nature." Kelley suggests that the exorcism procedure itself created an atmosphere which suggested a diabolical presence to the exorcist, as well as to the boy who was undergoing the rite. He notes: "As soon as the exorcism began, the boy started to have violent convulsions and to experience spells of unconsciousness." However, as we have seen, other sources state that the convulsions began earlier. Kelley adds that "at no time" during the St. Louis exorcism period "was the boy examined by physicians." To this might be replied that medico-psychiatric diagnoses had preceded the exorcism in Washington; still, according to the *Rituale Romanum*, these should probably have been repeated under ecclesiastical control in St. Louis.

The exorcism took place at a hospital operated by the Alexian Brothers. Each period of exorcism lasted for about and hour, and these took place once or twice a day. Often, the rites were held in the evening, because Douglass was at his most violent at night. Exorcisms consist of exhortation of the diabolical or demonic entity or entities; prayers, hymns, and forceful appeals for the entity to leave the possessed person's body. In contrast to his behavior at night, the boy was often quite pleasant during the day, and his relations with the members of the Alexian order became one of friendship. He was instructed in the Catholic faith; eventually, he and his parents became Roman Catholics.

Participants in the rites reported that the room in which the exorcism took place often had a "psychic chill," so that Father Bowdern had to wear an overcoat over his cassock and surplice. Douglass vomited often, and the room had to be cleared of vomit and stench regularly. Intravenous feeding was required to achieve some sort of nutritional regularity. When apparently under diabolic possession, the boy's face was distorted and his belly distended; his voice was rasping and strident. The Nicola account gives these details:

"As the exorcist recited the prayers, the lad began to spit intermittently onto his face with uncanny accuracy, invariably hitting the priest in the eye. One of the attending Jesuits held a pillow up between the exorcist and the boy as a shield.

It was at this point that the boy's tongue began to flick out and his head to move to and fro in the gliding fashion of a snake. Suddenly he would make a quick movement above, beneath and alongside the pillow and spit mucous into the exorcist's eye. Often during these attacks the boy appeared to be comatose. Meanwhile, regularly he delivered a barrage of insulting and offensive epithets at the exorcist and his aids, frequently accompanied by obscene gestures. On occasion he manifested an unfathomable knowledge of the sensitivities of the exorcist and others, attempting to create a feeling of distrust and hostility between them."

Throughout the months, the boy's mother had borne the emotional brunt of the ordeal. It was she who first observed the inexplicable phenomena in the boy's bedroom in Mount Rainier, and it was she who spent many hours with him in St. Louis during the days of the exorcism itself. Both she and Father Bowdern underwent severe emotional strains. Bowdern lost forty pounds in body weight during this period.

The decision to convert to Roman Catholicism led to baptism and to reception of the eucharist. According to Father Nicola, these were "the two wildest days in the entire case history." While the family was driving to church for the baptism, Douglass rode in the back seat of the car, between his uncle and his father, while the mother was driving. But the boy, managing to elude the grasps of the two men in the back seat, put his hands around his mother's throat. She had to pull her hands from the steering wheel, which permitted the car to crash into a lamp post.

Even in the church, prior to the baptismal rite, the boy was so unruly that the procedure had to be postponed. It took four hours until the baptism could be completed. Meanwhile, Douglass wrestled with the adults, threw himself to the floor, foamed at the mouth.

After the Lenten season, in April, Douglass grew markedly calmer. He awoke one day, saying he had a beautiful dream full of divine symbols. That afternoon, according to Nicola, a loud sound, like a shot, was heard in the hospital. This was during another of the boy's naps. He woke up, not knowing where he was or what had happened. Participants date his full recovery from that moment. The key phrase in the ritual used has been cited as follows:

"I command you, whoever you are, unclean spirit, and all your associates obsessing this friend of God, that by the mysteries of the Incarnation, Passion, Resurrection, and Ascension of Our Lord Jesus Christ, by the mission, the Holy Spirit and by the coming of the same Master, for the Judgment, give me your name, the day and the hour of your exit, together with some sign, and even though I am an unworthy minister of God, I command thee to obey in all these things nor ever again in any manner to offend this creature of God, or those who are here and any of their possessions."

Although, after all these years, the identity of the exorcist, Father Bowdern, and of other participants in the remarkable Washington-St. Louis case have been revealed, the true identities of Douglass Deen and of his family have remained secret. By now of course, Mr. Deen, whatever his real name may be, is a middle-aged adult; all that is known is that he does not live in either the Washington or St. Louis areas, that he has married, and is himself the father of teen-age children. Those who have spoken to him say that he seems to have genuinely forgotten the strange and fearful details that led up to, and extended throughout, his exorcism. Whatever demons or diabolical entities once controlled him, as a fourteen-year-old boy, are gone and have, for the most part, faded from his memory.

6. Celtic Nightmare

as told to Daphne Lamb

This is a travelogue with a difference: the historical beauty of Britain's Celtic countryside is marred by a horrid but unforgettable experience, the apparent possession of a little boy by an evil, seemingly demonic spirit entity. Ms. Lamb has based this report on an interview with a graphics designer who lives in New York City, but wishes to remain anonymous; all names have been changed. Daphne Lamb is a free-lance writer, amateur archaeologist, and close observer of social trends. She lives near Oxford, and is herself of Celtic descent.

Before I attempt to relate any of this I would like to go on record as saying that I have always been a sceptic. I believe neither in a conventional God nor in any of the trendier Gods who have so enraptured my friends and neighbors in the past decade. Exotic sects, whether they gather in the name of self-help or Satanic worship, leave me cold. I tend to believe in what is tangible, live by my own moral code (which is decent, I hope), and leave *occultomania* to those with the time and taste for dabbling in psychic phenomena. Having said that, I must beg you to believe that everything I am about to say is true, that—to the best of my knowledge and memory—I haven't tampered with any facts other than changing names. I have no explanation for what happened to my son during the summer of 1974 . . .

When Richard and I decided to take a month's holiday in Britain it was the fulfillment of a lifelong dream of mine. I had spent a week in London once as a part of my "grand tour" of Europe after I graduated from college, but I had never got beyond Windsor. What Richard and I both wanted was a leisurely tour of those mysterious areas the scholars refer to as Celtic Britain; we dreamed of the cliffs of Cornwall, the Welsh hills, the deeply indented coastline of western Scotland looking across to the Isle of Skye and the Outer Hebrides. We didn't have enough money or time to visit Ireland, too, so we contented ourselves with reading everything we could get our hands on concerning Celtic strongholds in Scotland, Wales, and the West Country. We pored over maps, planned our itinerary joyfully. We had decided to take our six-year-old son, Jamie, along with us. He was old enough to enjoy the trip and young enough for half-price accommodations in hotels. Every night before his bedtime I would tell him of the wonderful sights we'd see. I showed him pictures of ruined castles and Druidical Stones—all the things I had felt so inexplicably drawn to when I was an art student in college. Other girls might dream of the Coliseum by moonlight or Paris in the autumn; I fantasized about Stonehenge!

Richard was equally fascinated. He was himself of Welsh ancestry and could recall haunting stories told to him by his grandfather, who had emigrated from a village near Aberystwyth at the turn of the century. I suppose Jamie caught some of our excitement. At any rate, he was the sort of little boy who looked forward to every new experience with great zest. Open, friendly Jamie! I used to picture with heart-jolting anxiety situations in which my little son might jump into a stranger's car or strike up a cheery conversation with a maniac, but these particular urban nightmares did not come true. What did happen was so bizarre, so totally outside the realm of normal experience, that I have to force myself to go back over the details. Richard kept a sort of journal of those dreadful days. It started out as a travel journal, something to savor and reread when we returned to New York, but it ended up recording the horrible malady—I hesitate to call it by its right name—that turned our sunny six-year-old into a creature I could neither love nor protect . . .

The first five days of our holiday were spent in London, and they were the last moments of peace we were to know until we were once more suspended over the Atlantic on the homeward journey. It was early June, and the city was in a festive mood. Jamie loved the guards outside Buckingham Palace, the boatride up the Thames to the Tower, Regent's Park Zoo, and the toy department of Harrods. Everywhere he went he made friends. Even the staid, formidable salespeople in Fortnum & Mason smiled at him. The desk clerk at our Bloomsbury hotel hugged him and slipped a fivepence piece into his hand when we checked out. As I said, he was that kind of child.

We rented a car and set out for Cornwall, driving down through Wiltshire so we could stop off at Stonehenge on the way to the West Country. Jamie sat happily in the back of our Mini, chattering and pointing out cows, sheep, and interesting cars. His favorite was an Astin Martin we encountered near Winchester. It was early evening when we had our first glimpse of the Standing Stones. They rose starkly up from the green of the Salisbury Plain, looking so much as I had imagined them that I turned excitedly in my seat to point them out to Jamie. He was asleep. The hour was late and the turnstiles to the site were closed, so we turned into the village of Amesbury and took a hotel for the night. Jamie looked flushed and spoke in an uncharacteristic, fretful voice when I put him to bed, but I was so thrilled at the prospect of visiting Stonehenge in the morning that I took little notice. Jamie woke twice during the night, complaining of bad dreams, and in the morning he was flushed again, and surly. I took his temperature, which proved to be normal, and after breakfast we headed for the site, promising him he'd like it. He didn't.

FROM RICHARD'S JOURNAL

June 9: Stonehenge packed with German, French, and American tourists. Helen and I threaded our way through the camera-toting horde without Jamie. He announced that he didn't like the stones and stayed in the car, reading a comic book he'd picked up in the hotel lounge. Some of the ancient mystery came through, even in the crush, and Helen tried to explain to Jamie when we returned to the car. "Look," she said, "they're older than the pyramids." No reply. He put his hands over his eyes and wouldn't remove them until we had gone five miles. Not until we were deep into Somerset, heading for the splendors of Cornwall, did he recover his usual mood. "I *hated* those stones," he announced cheerfully. "Can we have some ice cream now?"

June 10: Drove into Cornwall from the North, along the coast. Jamie had a crying spell, first I can remember since he was a baby, as we approached the ruins of Tintagel Castle on the cliffs above the sea. We told him Tintagel was believed to be the ruins of King Arthur's Camelot, but he only turned away, sobbing. When we got out and walked along the cliffs he lagged back. Seemed afraid, and very pale. I stayed with him while Helen went down the steps carved in the cliffside to Merlin's Cave. A flock of gulls came wheeling over, screaming, and he began to scream too. At the hotel in St. Ives he seemed better, but complained in the night of bad dreams.

June 11: Lizard Point. The landlady here is a kind soul who offered to show Helen her Cornish magazines. At the back of each issue is a small index of Cornish words—there is a movement here to revive the language—and Helen tentatively tried to pronounce a few. Jamie ripped the magazine out of her hands and stamped on it. Landlady no doubt thinks he's a typical, spoiled, American brat. More bad dreams. He's still flushed, but doesn't have a fever.

Jamie picked up a bit when we left Cornwall. It was almost as if the rugged terrain of that most mysterious country depressed him. He hated the cliffs, the sea, the ancient stones on the hillsides; he drove through Bodmin Moor with clenched fists and a look of despair. When we pointed out a Druid "looking stone" high on a hill above the abandoned tin mines he narrowed his eyes and said: "I told you I don't like those f———ing stones." We were astonished. The last night we spent in Cornwall we summoned a doctor to the hotel. He examined Jamie and said he was probably overly tired. Jamie's eyes were glittering and overbright, his face flushed and dry to the touch. He was extremely rude to the doctor, muttering and grimacing. As Richard put it in his entry for that day: "The doctor tried to look amused when Jamie smashed his thermometer. Can this be our son?"

The farther we drove from Cornwall the more Jamie seemed his old self. In Bath he ate a huge dinner and dropped off to sleep immediately. "I've stopped dreaming about those stones," he announced with a look of relief. I was still worried—after all, his behavior had been so extraordinary—but after two blissfully uneventful days in Bath the memory had faded a bit. Jamie made friends with the publican's son in Bath and the two little boys played in the courtyard through the long, white twilight. Midsummer was approaching. It was time to head for Wales and our ultimate destination, Scotland . . .

June 14: Near Abergavenny. Jamie happy and companionable all day, until we crossed over into Wales. I noticed in the rear-view mirror that he had that flushed, feverish look again. Near a small village built on a steep hillside we almost had an accident. A ewe lay in the road, and when I stepped on the brakes to avoid hitting her, Jamie screamed. The ewe scrambled to her feet in confusion and ran straight toward the car. What with Jamie screeching and the long drive I put the car in reverse by mistake and nearly backed us off the road and into a little river. Jamie seemed to think this very funny—laughed and laughed. I must admit I felt like thumping him. When Helen said she was glad the ewe hadn't been hurt Jamie made the oddest sound. It almost seemed like another language. Whatever it was, it wasn't pleasant.

June 15: We're in a village about five miles from Aberystwyth, where my grandfather was born. Jamie barely slept last night—much tossing and crying out and dreaming. When Helen tried to comfort him he struck her hands away. I'd ask for a doctor again but I know what he'd say: Jamie's overtired. We plan to visit the Evanses, a very old couple who claim to remember Grandpa.

I remember the afternoon we spent with the Evanses so well that I still blush with shame at the memory. They were a lovely old couple, kind and eager to share their memories with Richard. They offered us tea and cakes and Jamie spat his Eccles cake out onto their table in a horrid mess and then went into a crying fit. Mrs. Evans offered to take him out into the garden. She took him by the hand and led him to the door and they disappeared for a moment. It was so still in the cottage kitchen that we could hear bees humming in the garden. I heard something else, too: a stifled gasp of pain from Mrs. Evans. She returned and made us some more tea, but she kept her hand hidden in her lap. Once she forgot and gestured, and I saw what I was looking for. A perfect crescent mark where Jamie had bitten her. The marks were deep; they must have hurt terribly. I was so ashamed. Richard recorded on that same day:

"Helen and I took turns visiting the churchyard where my ancestors are buried. Jamie screamed so loudly at the very idea that one of us had to stay in the car with him while the other made the pilgrimage. When I was with him, a little urchin from the village came up to the car and smiled at Jamie shyly. Jamie hissed—I can think of no other word that describes the sound accurately—and then said something incomprehensible to me. The little boy turned white and ran off. I can't tell Helen what I think because it sounds crazy. I think Jamie was speaking in Welsh. I think he said something terrible to the other boy."

June 16: Shropshire. We're back in England. This day has been a nightmare. Jamie was so hot to the touch when we drove through the enormous green hills of Snowdonia that I withdrew my hand instinctively. Still no sign of a fever. We bought a new thermometer in Betws-y Coed. Same results. Part of the time he almost seems to be in a coma. He shrieked a string of obscenities (some of them even shocked me) as we passed a churchyard on a hillside. He seems better tonight, but Helen and I feel we should consult a doctor when we reach Edinburgh.

The Edinburgh doctor was never to be. For one thing, both Richard and I had been dreaming so long of the West Coast that we decided to skip the city. Much more important—Jamie once again was in excellent spirits and seemed to have forgotten his outrageous behavior in Wales. When I tried to question him about what had happened with Mrs. Evans he looked so confused, so honestly bewildered and shocked, that I dropped it. He loved the Lake Country and began to look like the russet-cheeked little boys of Gainesborough paintings. He recovered his appetite and went "mountain climbing" with a crooked stick we had bought, in Cumberland, for a staff. Once again, my fears receded. I wanted so much to have the wonderful, memorable holiday we had planned that I purposely chose to forget the pall Jamie had cast over it in Wales and Cornwall. Understandable, I suppose, but a very stupid mistake. The worst was yet, as they say, to come . . .

June 19: Oban, Scotland. We have seen another doctor, here in this prosperous little fishing town. Jamie again feverish—in a terrible temper. He babbles fragments of things to himself continually. Our "leisurely" holiday has become frantic. We drove all day, not lingering to enjoy the lovely scenery, to reach a town where we thought we could get medical attention. The doctor was a very nice, fatherly type, who chuckled when we mentioned Jamie's bad dreams and said the "wee lad had most likely eaten too many sweets." He seemed amazed at the heat generating from Jamie's body but accepted the dictates of the thermometer without question. J. was sullen and uncommunicative, but there were no broken thermometers this time. As soon as we'd left the surgery, though, he began to laugh quite wildly. Something in his face repelled me. My own son.

The worst event of that endless night in Oban was not recorded in Richard's journal because he—exhausted—was asleep. It was I who woke up at 3 A.M. to the sounds of Jamie's screams. I leapt to his bedside and tried to rouse him, but the babbling I had come to fear only increased. I could understand occasional words, but most of it was in the strange nonlanguage he used so often now. It rose in pitch and continued—almost like a dialogue between two people— until I could bear it no longer. I slapped him, hard, to waken him, and made him sit up. When his eyes opened it was my turn to scream, because there was quite literally nothing there. I don't mean he'd rolled his eyes up so only the whites showed—I mean there was *nothing*. It was blank, empty, and I felt I was staring down a long corridor toward eternity. Before that moment I had feared (and repressed the thought) that my son might have a rare brain tumor, the sort which utterly changes the personality of the victim, but now a new fear possessed me. It was a fear of the Unknown. Sceptic that I was, I had no name for it.

June 20: We followed the curving road along Loch Linnhe, barely able to notice the splendors of the scenery . . . Helen red-eyed from lack of sleep; I on edge constantly. Jamie slept his unhealthy, comalike sleep in the back of the Mini. While he slept, Helen read to me from a guidebook she had purchased in Oban. We skirted Glencoe, the valley where the Clan MacDonald had been so cruelly massacred in the late seventeenth century, and as she read to me we became aware of a strange commotion in the car. We seemed to be rocking from side to side, although there was little wind. Jamie was twisting and turning in his supine position, thrashing about in the back seat like a beached fish, and the power of that small body in its grotesque throes was awesome. It seemed almost a convulsion, a cosmic one. Silently, Helen returned the book to the glove compartment and the commotion stopped. By tacit consent, we wanted to drive to a town written large on the map. We feared what we would once have welcomed—being stranded in a tiny, remote village with our son.

If we had thought Mallaig would be a metropolis, we were dead wrong. There were sheep grazing placidly on the lawn of our hotel. The main street of the town extended for only two blocks; most of the life of Mallaig centered around the port where boys of fourteen or fifteen sat mending fishing nets. A small fleet of boats bobbed vigorously on the choppy, North Atlantic waters. Jamie singled out one of the adolescent fishermen and said something to him in his strange new language which made the boy throw back his fair head and honk with laughter. I saw him later, and he looked at me with inexpressable contempt; I felt I had been raped. When we went to check in at the hotel, the sheep scattered as if we had pelted them with rocks. Even the gulls, ceaselessly circling, fled screaming out to sea at our approach. For the first time, there in Mallaig, Jamie made a definite request. He wanted to take the ferry to the Isle of Skye in time for Midsummer Night's Eve—the next day. How did he know such things? I was too tired to think properly. The awful noises which came from his bed each night kept me awake.

June 21: Raining dismally. We came by ferry from Mallaig to Armadale, in Skye, this morning. I do not know how to describe the events on board the boat. In point of fact, I don't want to. We are holed up in small hotel in the town of Portree. Don't know what to do . . .

I don't blame Richard for not wanting to set down on paper what happened on the ferry. I would forget it if I could . . . We carried Jamie, who was asleep, up from the bottom level where the car was stored, to the deck. It was still sunny, then, and I suppose I harbored vague, fatuous feelings about the therapeutic effects of sea air. We settled him between us and the boat churned out from Mallaig harbor into the strait separating the Scottish mainland from Skye. Jamie leaned heavily against me. In moments, I was asleep, and Richard decided to go below for coffee. I awoke because a dog who belonged to one of the passengers was barking hysterically. A woman plucked at my sleeve and pointed. There—sitting on the rail thirty feet above the rushing, deadly cold North Atlantic waters—sat my son. His body was arched backward, curved in a rigid parabola, as if he were about to let himself go over the rail. His eyes were closed; there was no expression on his face. One of the pursers was approaching him slowly, hands outstretched. Jamie's limbs twitched now and then; otherwise there was nothing to indicate that he was even alive. Everything seemed to move very slowly. Richard appeared on deck, two plastic cups of coffee in his hands. I saw his mouth open like an "O." The purser was almost next to Jamie when Richard bounded across the deck, seized Jamie by the heels, and brought him down to the safety of the boat's floor with a crash. The dog, I remember, whined in abject terror and scuttled away when Richard carried Jamie's body back to where I was sitting. The woman next to me muttered something about "fits," and Richard and I stared at each other numbly. We spent the rest of the voyage below decks, and when we drove off the ferry onto the Isle of Skye Richard's knuckles showed white on the steering wheel.

The rain began before we reached Portree. Jamie awakened, mumbling and crooning to himself, while we were negotiating a particularly narrow, steep length of road. In the rear-view mirror I could see his face, drawn and unbearably tense. His eyes were narrowed to slits. Time and again we skidded on the slippery mountain roads and I noticed that he smiled with satisfaction. The ghostly shapes of sheep ran before us in the mist—I remembered the ewe in Wales—and several times we had to slam on the brakes to avoid running into them. I began to feel that Jamie was willing us to crash. When we drove down the steep decline into the town of Portree I felt my life had been spared. I was no longer concerned for Jamie at that moment. I had been worrying, for the first time, about Richard and myself.

The rain stopped late that afternoon, and a feeble sun came out to illuminate the pale gray streets, the harbor lying in its protective circle of mountains, and the snake tree outside the window of the hotel's lounge. Jamie seemed to revive as the sun's rays crept into the dusty little room where we had been sitting, motionless and despairing, ever since our arrival. Our exhaustion was almost overpowering, yet neither Richard nor I felt we dared to sleep and leave Jamie alone. We ate an early supper in the hotel dining room, and once again Jamie's appetite was back to normal. Something else disturbed me, though. His manner toward us was sweet and friendly, but it was almost a parody of his old personality. His smiles were too gracious, his voice too cloying. He reminded us that it was Midsummer Night's Eve, and asked to go for a drive around the island now that the sun was out. We tried to beg off, explaining that it would soon be night, but Jamie countered—correctly—that it would be light until almost ten o'clock.

The further north we went, the longer the light held, and tonight was the longest night of the year. He got out the guidebook and pointed to pictures of marvelous cliffs, immense vertical stacks of striated rock standing guard over the sea, massive mountain ranges beckoning from the interior. There were other things to be seen, too: a bridge under which fairies congregated at twilight according to the old myths; a ruined castle which had belonged to MacDonald, Lord of the Isles. Jamie was irresistable in his pleas. I was still reluctant, but Richard was won over. We set out at 7 P.M., choosing the coastal road which looped unpredictably deep into the interior at times, only to circle back to the sea with unnerving subtlety. Jamie sat erect in back, pointing at interesting rocks and laughing with delight whenever another car approached. The roads were so narrow that one car was forced to huddle in a lay-by while the other crept past. You could see what was coming up the road from a long way off; the hairpin turns and deep hollows, combined with the extraordinary lucidity of the evening light, made visibility excellent.

I was watching Jamie in the rear-view mirror, fascinated by the expressions that flitted over his mobile features. He would smile secretively and then—catching my eye—broaden the smile until it seemed childlike and open. My hands were clenched in fists and my whole body felt extremely cold. Richard seemed unaffected. In fact, he was more at ease and happier than he had been for days. He and Jamie chattered and giggled and teased each other as in the old days, and a single, terrible thought ran through my mind, over and over: *He's won Richard over. He's won.* I didn't want to know what the words meant.

We were climbing steadily now. No cars passed us coming from the direction of the island's tip. Occasional flashes of sea appeared to the left, then the right. I felt disoriented, lost.

When Jamie shrieked a warning as we were rounding a sharp bend I intuitively braced my hands against the dashboard, yet there was nothing in our path. Richard only laughed. It happened twice more, until I no longer tried to protect myself. Then, as we emerged at the end of a long upward climb to a flat stretch of road, Jamie shouted again. An old man stood directly in our path, a bundle of peat on his shoulders. Richard braked sharply and I fell against the windshield, my forehead making sharp contact with the glass so that for an instant I saw the proverbial stars. I remember that Jamie cried my name anxiously. I didn't have to look to know that the expression on his face would be anything but anxious.

We were traveling along the sea now, high above the water, along the cliffs. Dizzying flashes of sheer drops flitted by; ahead we could see more sea, immense and very blue in the light of the midsummer sun. Signs appeared, red letters on white, proclaiming DANGER—STAY BACK FROM CLIFF EDGE. "Erosion," said Richard. "The cliff tops have eroded in a storm." Jamie snickered. "I wouldn't be afraid to walk there," he said persuasively. "Can't we stop?" Then I had to shut my eyes, because we were traversing the very lip of the island. The road wound along precariously. The sea lay 500 feet down, on our left. I had never been afraid of heights, but the terror I felt now was so deep and visceral I could not ignore it. If I was this afraid, there must be a reason. "Stop!" cried Jamie presently. "There's the castle." I felt the car slowing, heard the crunch of small stones under the wheels as Richard turned into a lay-by. Jamie was clamoring to get out and explore. "Look, Mommy," he wheedled, "there aren't any signs here. It's perfectly safe. Please, please!"

I opened my eyes. Richard was already halfway out the door. He and Jamie had eager, expectant looks on their faces. Fifty feet away loomed the ruins of a castle, jagged and desolate against the sky. And what a castle it must have been! No enemy could have attacked by water, no marauders could have scaled the cliffs to reach the fastness of the Lord of the Isles. It was built so precipitately atop the rock that it seemed merely a part of the cliff which plunged in a straight line down to the sea. Rocks thrust up like teeth from the churning water so far below; the blue water turned green and then broke in creamy white as if beat inward toward the circle of rocks. "Oh look," Jamie cried ecstatically, "it's beautiful!" He and Richard were already running across the bluff toward the castle; I mastered my terror and climbed out of the car on shaky legs to follow. After all, we were in this together, weren't we?

The wind was so fierce in this unprotected spot that my hair blew straight back like a flag. My ears began to ache with cold before I had taken ten steps. Jamie and Richard had reached the crumbling battlements and were climbing down onto some steps which had been carved into the cliffside. "Odd," I remember thinking, "that Jamie was so terrified at Tintagel and so unafraid now. Perhaps he's getting better?" A strange euphoria seemed to possess me at the thought. I ran toward them, climbing over the ruined walls without a trace of my earlier fear. The view was magnificent—the sea lay before us so vast and all-encompassing that it seemed to swim up over the horizon and fill my eyes. I felt so emotional that I couldn't be sure whether the tears on my cheeks had been whipped forth by the wind or had sprung up naturally at the sight of so much beauty. "Mom!" Jamie called, dancing over toward the edge of the stone steps. "Come here. It's great!" My feet seemed to move so lightly—I fairly flew toward him.

My memory of the incident is divided into two parts. The first is of the unnatural ecstacy I experienced—rather like what I have read of rapture of the deep—as I ran closer and closer to the edge. My little son was guiding me, telling me to come nearer. From far away I could hear Richard calling my name, but it didn't seem to matter. The second memory is unmatched, in my lifetime, for pure horror. Jamie was gone, gone. My guide had disappeared. I found myself teetering at the edge of the cliff, small rocks chipping away beneath my feet, only the sea before and beneath me. I dropped on all fours, clinging desperately to a hummock of turfy grass, lowering myself to my belly and feeling the world shift and swing around me. When Richard reached me I was afraid even to inch backward, to take his hand and walk away . . .

Neither of us spoke to Jamie on the long drive back. We felt we couldn't trust ourselves to communicate with him in any way. He had relapsed into his sullen, feverish persona, and as the darkness finally descended at 11 P.M. he seemed to lapse into a fitful sleep. We lurched along the narrow roads, skidding and inexplicably sliding from side to side, although the surface wasn't slippery. At one point we passed the old man who had stood in our path earlier; he was sitting motionless on a boulder by the side of the road. I couldn't bear to look at him. Sometimes I thought I saw fires high up in the hills, but when I looked again they were gone. We drove off the road on the long descent back to Portree, but Richard grimly wheeled back on course without even commenting. There was no explanation for what was happening. Both of us knew we'd be lucky to return alive, but neither would admit it. Richard's journal simply says: "There is no other way to put it. Jamie tried to kill Helen tonight. I saw it. We must return immediately."

It took us a long time to get to Glasgow, where we arranged to fly directly to Heathrow and then back to New York. The ferry from Skye plowed its way back to the mainland, Jamie, Richard, and I sitting below-deck the whole time. The drive back was agonizing. We had to go slowly, never taking our eyes off Jamie, who for the most part lay against the back seat alternately shivering with cold and burning up with fever. Never again did he speak to us in any way until we were airborne. We boarded the plane carrying him, like an invalid, between us. We told the stewardess that he had been taken ill in Skye and needed only to rest. He lay motionless for the first part of the trip, but I noticed that he stirred and seemed to be coming to life when the pilot announced we were flying over Yorkshire. At Heathrow he consented to eat a sandwich at the lunch bar, and then requested a large glass of milk. By the time we were flying over the Atlantic, Jamie was alert, cheerful, and totally normal again. We steeled ourselves for a return of what I had come to think of as his "other" self, but it never came.

We took him for a complete physical checkup when we'd been home for a few days and—as I'd suspected—there was nothing at all the matter with him. I told the doctor that he had undergone a total change of personality on holiday (leaving out the worst details) and was rewarded with a little dissertation on travel anxiety in six-year-olds. When Richard and I tried to broach the subject to Jamie himself it was like talking to a wall. He wanted to be cooperative, but he clearly couldn't imagine what we were talking about. Once, three weeks later, he came across a picture of Tintagel Castle. "Gee, Mom," he said, "why didn't we go there? It looks so neat." He remembered London, the Lake Country, the fun he'd had with the publican's son in Bath. Of the Celtic nightmares, not one impression remained.

Jamie is nine now. I've had three years to ponder the meaning of our aborted holiday, and still I can't arrive at a reasonable conclusion. I do not believe that children can become "possessed" by Satan; no matter how many films are made showing children vomiting green bile and speaking in tongues, I will not believe. What I have come—reluctantly—to believe is something almost as bizarre. I think that there are places on the earth which exert extremely strong influences over human beings who venture there. We may not even realize we are being swayed by the aura of a troubled spot—most of us are too sophisticated to separate such feelings from our normal, anxiety-ridden states—but it occurs nevertheless. Children, I believe, are particularly susceptible to the psychic waves emanating from ancient battlegrounds, "holy" places, or sites where great evil has been done; unlike adults, all their receptive channels are open and operating.

I think that an extraordinary transferrence occurred when Jamie first showed signs of horror at Stonehenge. My beloved Celts were a violent people—the greatest warriors of prehistory and firm advocates of blood sacrifice. Although scholars are divided in opinions as to whether human sacrifice ever occurred on the Salisbury Plains, it is certain that the Celts would not have scrupled to stain their altar stones with human blood. If Jamie was "possessed" when he set foot in those parts of Britain which had been the bailiwick of the Celts, then it was by a collective spirit of evil still lingering there. Some warp in the communal experience of mankind must have opened, allowing malevolent, demonic spirits to flood into the person of my innocent son. Once they had entered, Jamie was a receiving board, a magnetic field, which vibrated with malice whenever he approached the sites of ancient tragedies. It was certainly no accident that the worst of our horrors should have transpired where they did, and on Midsummer Night's Eve. Skye was thought to be the center of all witchcraft in the Middle Ages; at Midsummer the Hebridean skies were thick with flying sorcerers who came from all points of the globe for the Grand Coven. The castle on the cliff has always been a melancholy spot since the day—centuries ago—a hapless nursemaid allowed an infant

MacDonald to slip from her grasp and fall to his death in the sea below.

I am sure if I investigated further, I could find countless tales of sorrow, mayhem, and sorcery to reinforce my theory, but I shall have to leave that for someone less involved. I would prefer to forget.

7. Tu, the Avenger

Wilmon Menard

*The cross-cultural nature of the concept of demon possession
of children is vividly illustrated by the traditions of Polynesia.
Occasionally, elements that seem transplanted in time and
place surface in a modern setting; that is the case of the boy,
Tu, whom Mr. Menard encountered in Tahiti, and who appeared as an "avenger of the demon of darkness." Wilmon
Menard, author of a biography of W. Somerset Maugham,
lives in Hawaii and travels widely in the Pacific area.*

I first saw the Tahitian youngster Tu early one morning
when I drove into town from my beach-side house in the
Paea district. When I swung down to Papeete's tree-lined es-
planade that skirted the reef-encircled harbor, I saw him
seated on the sea wall holding a simple bamboo fishing rod,
hunched slightly forward, rigid, more like a small carved Polynesian *tiki*, or god.

Consulting the car's dashboard clock, I saw I was a half
hour too early for the opening of the post office, so I decided
to have a look at the youngster's catches, if any. He didn't
hear my sneakered tread as I came up behind him. A short
distance away I came to an abrupt halt. A strange low chant
was emerging from his throat, so ominous and unearthly that
I caught my breath sharply. It was not a boy's voice, but
deep and penetrating, and sonorous in tone, as if rising from
the bellowed-lungs of a giant islander. I remained transfixed,
scarcely breathing, ice water suddenly beading my forehead
and running down the rib cage from my armpits.

The awesome chant was like nothing I had ever heard before, neither in any eucharistic liturgy or from a ritual witch

doctor of darkest Africa. The effect was unnerving, deeply disturbing to my otherwise complacent and logical approach to the occult, the supernatural, the parapsychological manifestations to which an outsider is constantly exposed in Polynesia, although most times these turn out to be erroneous, exaggerated rumors, or the alcoholic hallucinations of a local boozer. But here was something different, quite different, indeed! This innocent-looking boy had not learned this chant in any mission church or schoolroom. It was from far out of Polynesia's heathen past, when fierce stone gods lined the shores of this island, when slaughtered victims were laid out on the altars of *maraes* (platforms of stone temples), and huge double canoes of the infamous *Arioi* Society—the cult of witchcraft worshipping ghosts and gods of terror and vengeance—set sail for the atoll of Tetiaroa, 25 miles distant from Tahiti, for their diabolical meetings of black magic and *pifao* (death curses). Movie actor Marlon Brando is now the owner of this once sacred and *tabu* isle, where ruins of the pagan *maraes* can be seen today.

Yet, as I stared fixedly at the innocent features of this boy's face, the crisp ringlets of hair catching the rays of the early morning sun, his slightly oversized shorts and bare feet dangling close to the calm clear lagoon, there was nothing to distinguish him markedly from the groups of students now passing in the road behind on their way to the schoolrooms of the Catholic brothers. Especially now that his chanting had ceased. The rigidity had gone from his body, as if in disarming awareness that some alien presence was close, an intruder, an eavesdropper, perhaps an enemy, who should be put off guard by casual aloofness.

The spell was broken. I heard again the early morning sounds of the aroused port of call: church bells tolling distantly in liquid tones, roosters lustily crowing behind in the valleys still wreathed in mists; motor scooters with passengers in tandem, most times attractive shapely *vahines*, their long hair flying in the wind, jockeying for lead positions in their wild races for coffee and croissants before starting another workday in the shops and government offices; the glass-bottom launch for the tourists moving languidly with low growl of engine propulsion across the opalescent lagoon toward the refueling jetty; a taxi filled with revelers, speeding past toward the country districts below Papeete, a brief punctuation of guitar music and happy singing. The blue sea mists were rising from the island of Moorea, twelve miles across the Tahiti channel. The tight constriction in my chest eased somewhat, and my breathing became more normal.

"Catching anything?" I asked the solitary boy quietly.

His head turned slowly, the eyes raised to my face, almost without focus, as if in a trance. He was a handsome youngster, with the Greek-like perfection of facial planes one sees so frequently throughout Polynesia, the eyes large, dark, and guileless, although now of odd lackluster expression, as if awakened from a sleep of perplexing dreams.

He shook his head just once, and then turned away, at the same instant lowering the line of his fishing rod deeper into the water. But not so artfully that I didn't catch a brief glimpse of the startling object, weighted with a small stone, that he had been dangling just below the surface of the lagoon. It was a small crudely carved figure, an effigy in the shape of a boy or girl! In Haiti such an effigy might be used by a witch doctor for piercing with needles, burning, or various forms of mutilation. In French Polynesia, in the pagan era, a *tahua*, or priest, would offer such a token replica of a selected villager, fallen under a *pifao* (death curse), to the vengeance of a drowning death decreed by the Shark God of the Sea, Ta'aroa.

But this was 1977, not the fifteenth century!

The island boy took no notice of me again, and, from his seemingly mesmerized staring at the fishing line angled down into the blue lagoon, he had shut me out of his mind; I had ceased to exist for him.

"Well, whatever it is you're fishing for, good luck," I said lamely.

I doubt if he heard me. I walked back to my car.

As I was about to turn the key in the ignition, there was the thin tooting of a motor scooter's horn from the rear of my car. I glanced in the rear-view mirror. A Tahitian friend of mine—a male teacher in one of the district schools, with whom I occasionally went deep-sea fishing—had braced the Vespa and was walking up to my side.

After Viri and I had shaken hands, he announced in French rather gravely: "I saw you talking to that boy there as I was going past, so I circled around and came back." He lifted his head and glanced over the top of the car to the motionless form on the sea wall. "What do you make of him?"

"I'm afraid not very much. He doesn't exactly communicate. But as a quick appraisal, I'd say he's a rather withdrawn little chap, and doesn't encourage any gesture of friendship. A real loner, who prefers his own private world."

He stared at me for a few moments, and his expression was of extreme agitation. Then he blurted out: "Yes, yes, indeed! He does have 'his own private world'—and not a very good world, I can tell you!"

"What's that supposed to mean?" I asked.

Viri shook his finger nervously for emphasis, as he said in a low tense voice: "I know that boy, and there's something not of this world about him! He has a look in his eyes . . . he sits for hours sometimes staring out to sea, doing nothing. Then I've come across him doing strange things with some objects he keeps hidden in the pandanus bag he carries over his shoulder, all the time talking to himself or with someone he imagines can hear him. It's an unhealthy way for such a small boy to spend his time." His eyes shifted uneasily back to the sea wall, then he gripped my arm. "Come along with me for coffee. I don't like to talk about him here. I'm sure he's listening, even at this distance."

My interest aroused, I followed him to the small restaurant of Papeete's Rue Paul Gauguin. Seated, and our order placed, he leaned forward, talking rapidly in almost a whisper. "It upsets me very much to even speak of that boy. His name is Tu. Now, if you know your Tahitian history, the High Chief Tu was the first king of these islands. He came from the Tua-motu Archipelago, which as you know is just northeast of here, and his ancestor was a shark god, at least so our *para-pores* (legends) say. Anyway, this first King Tu was the founder of the Pomaré royal family of Tahiti."

"How does all this relate to the boy?" I wanted to know.

"He is named for this Tu of the Tuamotus. And this boy's great-grandfather was Hiro-Tu, a hereditary *tahua* (priest) of Tahiti. The boy was actually born in the island of Manga Reva of the Gambier Group, on the edge of the Tuamotus, not too far from Easter Island. And that island, I can tell you, is an island of bad *tupaupaus* (ghosts). Go to the *Musée* here in Tahiti if you want to see some of the pagan objects that have come from Manga Reva. So, now you can perhaps understand why that boy you spoke to on the sea wall acts so abnormally, why he never plays with the other boys of his own age, why he is always walking along the beaches by himself, wandering here and there, sleeping in odd places."

"Doesn't he have a home here, a relative?" I asked.

"Oh, yes, he was sent from Manga Reva six months ago to live with a distant family of relatives, to go to school. But he keeps running away, and my friend who teaches in Mataiea has him in his class, and he says the boy comes and goes as the whim seizes him. He says he's a very distractive influence. The other students don't like him, and seem frightened of him. At first they teased this Tu about his Manga Revan accent, but no more. They soon learned he is not a boy to taunt. Not that he is physically aggressive, because he isn't, it's just the way he looks at them, the unspoken menace that seems to radiate from him. It's all very uncanny, believe me."

I told him about the carved wooden figure I had glimpsed on the end of his fishline, and I heard him take a sharp catch of breath.

"*Mon Dieu*, so that's what he was doing there!" he exclaimed. "Such heathen things have not been done here in French Polynesia for hundreds of years! He should be sent back to Manga Reva to his immediate family! Tahiti is no place for a boy such as he!" He swallowed hard in his inner agitation. "*Certainement*, he is possessed by the evil gods of our heathen past!"

I was suddenly remembering the burning of the "witches" of Salem, on Gallows Hill, not far from my birthplace of Beverly in Massachusetts. Poisonous rumors, pointing fingers, secret meetings, peerings through windows, skulking figures stalking suspect "possessed" persons. A community gripped by superstition and fear, the mania mounting and spreading, bursting into hysteria to cause the slow cremations of women, whose only crime was perhaps that of eccentricity.

In a mollifying tone, I said: "I don't think it's a good idea to get all worked up about this. Imagination and rumor can run riot on a situation like this. This boy Tu is just perhaps a very lonely boy, no doubt hypersensitive, who insulates himself by a studied strangeness and detachment. There are perhaps many reasons why he's a loner with the other boys his age. I know how cruel children can be. I figure he's been kicked around a lot among his relatives, who haven't taken the trouble to understand him, give him love, help him. Deep down he could be very unhappy and disturbed."

"I understand what you're saying," the school teacher said

shortly. "But this Tu's case is different, very different, indeed!"

I chose not to think so. Still, I remembered the uneasiness I experienced standing beside Tu on the sea wall.

My teacher friend Viri finished his coffee hurriedly, mumbled something about being late for his classes, and with a rather tight-lipped expression took his leave. He seemed annoyed that I chose not to accept his suspicions of the boy Tu. As I watched him stride off, I thought: Either his imagination is running away with him, or he's reverting in this circumstance to the origin of his Polynesian strain, a race that for centuries, and still today, holds strongly to their superstitious beliefs.

Little did I know!

I saw Tu a few times after our first encounter on the sea wall, sometimes sitting motionless under a tree a short distance along the road out of town, now walking along a back street of Papeete, again on a bus headed for the districts on the west or south coast of Tahiti. He was always alone, the expression on his face neither sad or happy, detached, never seeming to notice any person or incident taking place close to him. He seemed to have no playmates, he never joined in any games, nor did I once see him in the group of boys and girls who frolicked in the lagoons. People, young and old, avoided him, particularly the Tahitians; the stares of the tourists and Chinese storekeepers he didn't seem to be aware of, nor did he seem conscious of how Tahitians circled widely around him in the street, or crossed to the other side rather than pass him. I felt sorry for him, convinced that a pervasive Tahitian ostracism, with no valid justification other than pure Polynesian ghost gossip, had been viciously mounted against him, causing him to feel alone, unwanted, and rejected.

Once, driving out of town to my home, I passed him at the start of the Punaauia district, walking slowly at the side of the palm-shaded roadway. I tooted the horn and slowed down, motioning an invitation of a ride to wherever he was going. He turned full face and glared at me, and I was rendered speechless by the look of hatred in his eyes. I shrugged my shoulders and drove on. No doubt about it, he *was* an abnormal youth!

Then a tragic event, which subsequently was to involve the boy Tu, took place. An inter-island RAI plane, on a flight out of the Faaa Airport, crashed on the barrier reef of Raiatea

Island, 125 miles or so northwest of Tahiti. There were few survivors. A few days later, my schoolteacher friend Viri drove up my short driveway, and behind riding tandem, was another Tahitian, whom he introduced as a substitute schoolteacher of the Mataiea district on the southern coast of the island. My friend was in great agitation, out of breath from excitement, and it was only after he had sat down, inhaling deeply a few times, was he able to speak coherently.

"The RAI plane that went down at Raiatea! . . . a terrible thing!" he gasped. "The boy Tu caused that to happen!" When he saw the baffled expression on my face, he exclaimed to his friend: "Tell him . . . tell him what you know!"

The schoolteacher of Mataiea spoke quietly, but his inner turmoil was revealed in his hands, which he kept twisting nervously together, and the shocked expression in his eyes.

"This Tu of Manga Reva is supposed to attend my classes, but he comes only as he likes. A little girl named Tetua sat behind him. She was the one who mimicked him the most, always teasing him. There is no *g* or *k* in the Tahitian language, but there is in the Gambier tongue of Manga Reva. She was forever bedeviling him, talking the way he did, making faces at him, all to amuse her playmates. Once, when in the school yard during recess he grabbed her by the throat, the power in his fingers was incredible. He shook her with the strength of a strong man. Her friends attacked him, beating him with sticks until he let go. Then they chased him away down the beach, yelling *'Tamaiti-ti'aporo! Tamaiti-ti'aporo!* Devil-boy! Devil-boy!' "

Ah, I thought, now we're getting to the basis of Tu's estrangement, the persecution that had its inception with his school companions, a common cause of nervous disorders which some carry with them into adult life.

The Mataiea teacher continued: "That night this little girl Tetua was discovered in bed, rigid, froth bubbling from each corner of her mouth, eyes bulging with fright."

"Epilepsy?" I asked casually.

"No, no, not at all! She has no history of such. A native *tahua* (priest) was called in, and he performed the ancient rites of exorcism. The girl was saved."

"What has all this to do with the plane crash at Raiatea?" I interrupted.

"This Tetua was supposed to be on that flight to Raiatea to visit with a *fetii* (relative) in the village of Fetuna. But at the last minute her mother brought her back. She said she had a vision of the plane falling and breaking up on the reef."

"Now, you see why I say this boy Tu is possessed!" exclaimed Viri.

"I would say it's just a strange coincidence," I said impatiently.

Viri exchanged an exasperated look with his friend. "You see, I told you, he cannot be convinced. He is a *popaa* (outsider) who just deals in cold logic. I suppose that is why he is an outstanding anthropologist."

"I just can't accept seriously all the stories I hear in these islands about your spirit world," I retorted. "Most of them are old women tales, with no basis of fact or credence."

Viri now spoke earnestly: "We were hoping you'd be convinced of the menace of this boy Tu, to speak with some of your friends in the Government here, so the possessed one could be sent back to his island of Manga Reva where he belongs among the *sacré* ruins and ghosts and *tikis* there. They would listen seriously to you."

"I'm not entering into any vicious conspiracy, based on the flimsy premise of gossip, to harm this boy. If you spent as much time trying to help him, rather than persecuting him, you might be able to reach him, to let him lead some sort of a normal life here." I was highly indignant at their suggestion.

The two stood up. Viri shook a reproving finger in my face. "Just wait! Just wait!" he exclaimed angrily. "You will live to regret the opportunity you had to help us send this Tu away from here!"

They stalked out sullenly.

A week later I received the shocking news that the little girl Tetua had drowned off the reef passage of Mataiea, while paddling in a small outrigger canoe with companions. She was the only one lost, the others swimming easily to the reef. Her body was recovered in an underwater grotto, badly mutilated by sharks and conger eels.

I felt compelled to speak to a missionary in Papeete of the Catholic Order of Picpus, who at one time had been stationed at the old cathedral in Rikitea of Manga Reva. He was old and gray-bearded and a little deaf. He seemed to know why I had sought an audience with him.

"Oh, yes, yes, I know of the boy Tu," he said in a tired voice. "There is an evilness in that poor boy. It is not his fault, you understand, for being possessed by a Satanic spirit. The Church, of course, recognizes the circumstance of possession."

"But haven't you tried to help him?" I asked, surprised by his seeming indifference. "Is he so far out of your realm of influence?

The old priest patted my shoulder in the indulgent gesture by which a father might restrain a son's heedless words. "Some possessed ones can be saved, others cannot. There's a limit to what the Church can accomplish in these things."

"Didn't his father, on Manga Reva, take any interest in the boy . . . couldn't he control him?"

"The father was a big, strong Polynesian," replied the priest. "He worked as a pearl diver at Hikueru Atoll in the Tuamotu Archipelago during the diving season for shell. His strength was in his lungs and limbs, not in his brain. He beat the boy all the time, sometimes with his huge bare fists as if he was his equal in size and age. Once, drunk, he tried to crush his son's head with an iron-wood club."

"Good God!" I gasped. "Why wasn't something done to stop the father's brutality? No wonder the boy is peculiar, an outcast!"

"My son, the father claimed he was driving the Devil from his son. In his native ignorance he thought violence was the best way."

"He should be in jail for what he's done to his son!"

The priest's head came up slowly on a level with mine, his eyes sought mine, held, and before speaking his lips trembled slightly. "He has now gone to his own place of incarceration. The boy's father, as I told you, was a diver for pearl shell. He met his death far below the lagoon of Hikueru. His foot, either by accident . . . or from some other cause . . . slipped into the furbelowed shells of a giant clam. Sharks always gather when there is a helpless fish or human. They attacked before the other divers could rescue him." He sighed heavily. "There were not sufficient remains for a proper burial." Then, bending forward, labored, with throaty hoarseness, he added: "And the boy Tu knew that his father was dead, long before the news reached Manga Reva!"

I was gripped by conflicting emotions on my drive back to Paea, while trying to separate fantasy from logic. One thing I was determined to do. The priest had given me the name of

Tu's guardian in the district of Mataiea. I would investigate what sort of a home life he had there with his relatives.

Two days later, in the early afternoon, I drove up to a small wooden house set back in a grove of palms and breadfruit trees off the beach. I heard the wild shrieking of a woman above the sound of my engine, an unearthly banshee howling that catapulted me from the car for a hard race around a corner of the dwelling.

An awesome and revolting scene greeted me. There in the clearing, margined by hibiscus and oleander bushes, just below the small front veranda, a huge Tahitian woman, her *pareu* (sarong) and long black hair still dripping with seawater from a swim in the lagoon, was struggling with the boy Tu. The volume of rage exploding from her throat had reached the peak of a crazed crescendo. The unequal physical encounter was shocking. Her strong fingers had embedded themselves in his long thick hair, and with amazing leverage she had dragged him across the slanted trunk of a palm tree. With her massive free arm she was punishing him, delivering powerful open-hand blows to the face and across bare chest and shoulders. Tu's nostrils were streaming blood and gore was welling between split lips, but no sound of protest came from him, no whimper of pain or entreaty. What stunned my sensibilities was how his eyes looked. There was no expression, or reaction, to his cruel ordeal, only a fixed staring, as if focused on something very far away and unrelated.

"Son of the Devil! Excrement of a ghost!" She was screaming in Tahitian. "You made my hair snag in the branching coral underwater! You stood there on the beach, watching, smiling, as I almost drowned! You wanted me to die, like the little girl Tetua!"

Suddenly she reached behind her and snatched up an iron bar with a sawtooth circular end, used to grate coconut. I yelled warningly and rushed in. Before she could land the murderous blow, I had clamped a firm grip on her wrist, twisting and throwing her off-balance at the same time. She fell heavily on her back, grunting her surprise, dragging Tu completely with her across the base of the palm. Squirming, he freed his hair of her entwined fingers, and was up and away in desperate flight.

"What are you trying to do?" I shouted down at her. "Kill the boy, is that what you're trying to do?"

She rose to her heavy haunches, swaying slightly, brushing

back the disheveled hair from her contorted face, inhaling spasmodically through clenched teeth.

"You get out of here!" she snarled in French. "What business is it of yours? That devil-boy almost killed me with the help of the black spirits in him! I was trying to drive the *Varua-ino-Po* from his possessed soul!" She was struggling now to get to her feet, perhaps to attack me. "Do you know what the *Varua-ino-Po* is, you bastard *popaa* (outsider)?"

Yes, I did. The *Varua-ino-Po* was the Tahitians' dread Bad-Demon-of-Darkness!

"If I hadn't interfered you would have killed the boy with that weapon," I said coldly. "A crime that would have surely sent you to prison."

She was on her feet now, holding to a palm tree for support, breathing heavily to regain her strength, and still berating me.

"You are trespassing, you understand that, you stupid foreigner! You get off my property right now, or I will throw you off! And if you dare step foot on here again I will call the *mutoi* (district policeman), and he will take you to jail!"

She followed behind me, staggering heavily, heaping verbal abuse, as I returned to my car.

"What do you know about the trouble that *sacré* monster has caused me, you imbecile?" she yelled. "The boy is only distantly related to me, but I accepted him into my house! Now, for my charity I am treated like a leper by my neighbors here in Mataiea! There is no more friendliness in this district. The men and women here no longer dare to go out night fishing, they hide in their *fares* (huts) with a light burning, so frightened are they of this boy-devil." She shook a huge fist at me. "And you stopped me from beating the evilness from his soul!"

As I drove away she was still shaking her fist after me, a challenge again to return and face her in physical combat.

A few times along the roadway, for five miles or so, I stopped to make a limited reconnoiter to see if I could sight Tu, in case he was in need of emergency first aid from his brutal chastisement at the hands of his giantess guardian. The coconut groves and stretches of beach were deserted. No doubt, the boy had gone into hiding in one of the heavy foliaged valleys, where he could subsist on native vegetables and fruits growing wild and a fresh water stream. I felt a deep commiseration for this abused boy, who had only known hostility and cruelty in his short lifetime. I still refused to believe he was possessed by a Polynesian demon.

A few days later, my schoolteacher friend, Viri, stopped me in town to inform me: "The people of Mataiea have made a very careful search of the district, but they can't find a trace of the boy Tu. They are convinced he is no longer there. But if he is located in any other district, they will insist he be sent back to Manga Reva."

Two months passed, with still no clue as to the where-abouts of the fugitive Tu. Eventually, my concern for him lessened in the course of my anthropological field trips around the island and in the outlying isles of the Leeward and Austral Groups. I hoped he had found a sort of sanc-tuary in one of the hidden valleys, where it would be possible for him to come into young adulthood, able to fairly defend himself against the inhumanities of superstitious villagers.

Then, when the memory of Tu had almost faded from my mind, I received the startling news that the boy's guardian had died a strange death in her sleep. Viri came by my house in Paea to give me details.

Seated beside me on the lagoon-side veranda, with the dramatic silhouette of Moorea Island on the horizon, it took him a few minutes, and half of a tumbler of rum, to com-mence his account, so intense was his agitation.

"The woman Purea, the boy's guardian, had gone to bed early after a light dinner with her niece who was visiting her from Bora-Bora. She was in good health and spirits. Then, close to midnight, the niece heard her cry out in a terrible voice of fright. At the same time, she remembered, a cold blast of wind had swept through the house, causing the half curtains in the doorways to fly wildly, and chairs, tables, and dishes to crash to the floor. And there was an oppressive odor, like one finds of mould and decay around our _maraes_.

"Finally, the niece overcame her fright to venture into her aunt's bedroom. She found her halfway sprawled out of bed, not breathing, quite dead, and with the most horrible look on her face, as if she had seen before her end a soul-shattering glimpse of our _Te Po_ (Region of Darkness, or Hell) and the demons who dwell there."

I interrupted him with the casual remark: "She was a very heavy woman. She could have suffered a cardiac arrest."

Viri shook his head vehemently. "No, no, not at all! The autopsy revealed no organic ailments. And she had no medical history of any illnesses. Her death was caused by strangulation and traumatic shock."

I stared at him incredulously. "Are you trying to tell me she was choked to death?"

He replied quietly: "Yes, by a *tupaupau* (ghost) of the *Varua-ino-Po*, using the boy Tu as the earthly assassin." He arose and looked down at me with a speculative expression. "I know that in your scientific mind you are readying a sort of logical solution to all that has happened here because of the presence of the Manga Reva boy in this island, but, as a Tahitian, I can tell you in all frankness that in Polynesia there is such a thing as the possession of the soul of mankind by horrible phantoms who dwell in the spirit world-of-darkness."

He left me more troubled in mind that I cared to admit.

And I was sure that now there would be an intensive hunt for Tu, that would continue until he was found, if he actually were still hiding somewhere in the island. He would be chased down by men, women and children, led by packs of ferocious pig-hunting dogs—and when they found him he would be torn to pieces in the traditional destruction of a mortal believed to be possessed of a demon of the *Varua-ino-Po*.

A few weeks following the death of his guardian, I began to be less concerned about Tu. The search had brought no results. I was certain he was clever enough to have found an inviolable, well-concealed lair. And, for all anyone knew, the fugitive boy had managed to stow away on a trading vessel for his birthplace island of Manga Reva.

But I was to make a grisly discovery one afternoon on a return drive from a field trip to Tautira on the southern peninsula of Tahiti. Passing through the district of Mataiea, I decided to make another visit to the Great Marae of Mahaiatea, going down a branching road flanked by a small community of new homes, and then alongside a tree-shaded area with a massive mound of coral rubble and boulders. What once had been one of the most sacred stone temples of Tahiti consisted now of only the base of a section of its side walls. A barrier reef, usually a mile or so out, protects Tahiti's almost entire coastline, but at this *tabu* site, the coral reef encroached closer to shore, and the tumult of the pounding surf was nerve-racking. By a strange whim of the sea gods, two opposing currents collided here with white-crested waves, immediately in front of the *Marae*, creating a cauldron of froth. It was not a place of sacred rest, where the spirits of the Marae's victims or the priestly guardians could ever have found eternal peace. The conflict of the sea here was too violent.

I remembered Captain James Cook's description of the Marae of Mahaiatea. He had been overwhelmed by its magnitude and sacred atmosphere, calling it simply "Wonderful!" Then it had been an immense Tahitian pyramid of carefully arranged blocks of stone and coral, in a series of stepped-back ascents, almost fifty feet high and 270 feet long. In the center of its summit rose the ominous figure of a spirit bird carved in wood and a leaping fish chiseled from stone. And scattered all about were human bones of victims sacrificed to the Polynesian god Oro.

Now, just a gigantic altar of tumbled rocks!

I made a precarious climb to the top of the mound of stones and rubble. The roar of the sea here was even more tumultuous. Then I saw something, wedged halfway down the heathen barrow in a crevice of this ancient and forbidding monument to pagan idolatry. What was it? The small bleached stump of a tree trunk, the mummified carcass of a wild pig, an accumulation of coconut husks?

I cautiously made my way down to investigate. Then, a short distance from my objective, I stopped short, throwing myself back against the rocks with a gasp of horror! It was the corpse of a young boy—and it was Tu! The blazing sun and sea air had partially shriveled the pathetic remains. I huddled for what was only minutes, but seemed an eternity, against the uneven tier of stones. My throat was constricted, mouth dry with the effect of shock, heart pounding violently, causing a cold sweat to stream down my limbs.

What hellish impulse had diverted my homeward trip? What infernal machination of occult force had compelled me to clamber up this mound of relic rocks to involve myself in such a gruesome find?

What was so macabre and blood-chilling was what I had seen protruding from the small rib cage. It was a length of stag coral, deeply embedded in the vicinity of the heart, with the dark stain of what had once been human blood dry smeared now on the stark-white petrified spurs.

Slowly, carefully, lest I start a small rock avalanche, I descended the mound, panicked thoughts chasing one another through my brain. Was Tu's death an accident, or deliberate homicide? Had he imprudently, through hunger, braved the malestrom of the ocean's whirlpool off his refuge seeking sea life, when a sudden powerful undersurge of the sea hurled him against a live and poisonous outcropping of coral? His chest critically pierced, had Tu's last desperate act been to crawl ashore, seeking a final crypt of sacred stones for a solitary death? Or had some anonymous hereditary *tahua* (priest) of today's Tahiti dealt the sacrificial death blow at this ancient pagan site?

It will perhaps always remain a mystery.

I didn't report my discovery of Tu's mutilated corpse. But a month later I did return to the Marae of Mahaiatea to reaffirm to myself that what I had witnessed had not been a ghastly hallucination.

No trace remained of the small ravaged cadaver, just the spurred javelin of stag coral glistening in the sun against the black rocks, like the cast aside and broken instrument of death of a sea god of Polynesia.

8. The Poltergeist Child

D. Scott Rogo

Modern parapsychology does not accept the hypothesis that unexplained physical phenomena in the vicinity of a child are the result of demon action; nor do parapsychologists any longer assume that such "poltergeist" phenomena are caused by a "ghost" (Geist means "ghost" in German), but may emerge from unresolved emotional conflicts that find destructive physical outlets. Mr. Rogo is a California parapsychologist and musician, author of several books, including the recent A Century of Phantoms.

Chris was probably the most gifted child psychic I ever encountered. Yet I doubt if she knew it. In fact, I doubt that she realized at all that she was psychically responsible for the outbreak which had caused objects to fly by themselves throughout her mother's house. She was, simply speaking, a "poltergeist child."

The poltergeist is one of the most eerie and fascinating forms of psychic phenomena. Roughly translated from the German, the word *poltergeist* means "noisy ghost." Poltergeists (also called Recurrent Spontaneous Psychokinesis, or RSPK) create brief disturbances which resemble what one might encounter while staying in a more conventional haunted house. A family victimized by a poltergeist will suddenly confront some unseen force which raps on household walls, throws objects about, smashes crockery, breaks windows, dematerializes objects, and sometimes even sets fires. When the poltergeist erupts, literally all hell breaks loose. The poltergeist usually concentrates on one member of the household. Often, this agent is a child. The disturbances will focus on this individual, either attacking him the most violently and viciously, or will only occur when he is present in the house. If he leaves or goes to sleep, for instance, the poltergeist will usually abate. However, his return or awakening will arouse the poltergeist once more. Luckily, though, poltergeist attacks are rather short in duration and rarely last more than a month or so.

These facts about the poltergeist have been known for years. Even in the 1890s, psychical researchers wondered why children always seemed to be present when the poltergeist struck a household. One explanation was obvious to them. Perhaps, they thought, these children were slyly faking the rackety and ghostly disturbances. On the other hand, some of the more enlightened investigators felt that perhaps there was an intricate psychic relationship between the minds of these children and the poltergeist itself. But . . . just what kind of relationship? Today, we know a great deal more about the poltergeist and poltergeist children than the psychical researchers of the 1890s did. So, now, for the first time, we might be able to answer this question.

In many poltergeist cases, it looks as though these children are harboring masses of repressed hostility, frustration, and guilt. In other words, deep within their minds are hostilities and angers which they cannot express consciously or verbally. As these frustrations grow, they seek expression. Could it be that these children are using PK (which stands for "psychokinesis," or "mind over matter") to vent their frustrations? This seems likely. I am sure that everyone has seen how a child will act if angered by his parents, playmates or—when older—boyfriends or girlfriends. He or she will slam doors, throw things, break things, kick the dog, or pound on the walls in fury. These are just the sort of acts which the poltergeist carries out as well. It, too, bangs doors, throws things, and breaks everything in sight. (Yes, there are even a few cases of dogs being kicked!) So, it looks as though the poltergeist is not really a ghost at all. It is, instead, a type of disturbance employed unconsciously by a person when he cannot express his frustrations in any normal way. The poltergeist does it for him.

Chris was a typical poltergeist child. She was thirteen, but looked much older, had beautiful blond hair, and was stunningly attractive. She looked more a mature teen-ager of seventeen than a mere child hardly into adolescence. I first met her in 1974 when a local psychical research society in Los Angeles phoned my colleague, Raymond Bayless, to report that they had received word of a poltergeist-afflicted home in a nearby community. By early that evening, Raymond and I were at the house trying to help the family through the ordeal they were facing.

The poltergeist was rambunctious enough, that's for sure. When I first arrived at the house (Raymond arrived a bit later), Chris, her mother, and her aunt, were sitting out on the front lawn. They were too frightened to go inside, but I finally coaxed Chris, the most venturesome of the three, to escort me in through the back door. No sooner had we walked through the kitchen and into the living room than I heard what sounded like small objects being hurled about upstairs. I ran to investigate, leaving Chris behind. Nothing happened while I held my short vigil, but when I returned to the living room I heard another object thrown upstairs. Chris couldn't stand it any longer, and ran from the house screaming and crying at the same time.

Raymond and his wife arrived at the house right after this brief but impressive episode. He, too, was able to coax Chris and her relatives back into the house and settled them in the kitchen before going upstairs to confer about the situation with me. No sooner had we gone upstairs and entered a bedroom to talk when we heard an incredible bang. We ran to the stairway landing instantly, and I watched with fascination as a glass bottle bounced down the stairs. It had apparently struck the heater at the top of the stairs, which would account for the loud metallic bang we had heard. As we watched the bottle topple to the floor, I could hear the family members talking animately in the kitchen which was situated at the other side of the house. Could one of them have thrown the bottle, I wondered? I doubted it, but couldn't be sure.

If I had any doubts about the authenticity of the poltergeist by that time, they were shattered that evening. After the flurry of PK that had greeted me upon my arrival, silence reigned for quite a while. In fact, Raymond was using the lull to set up accommodations for himself and his wife when the next antics broke out. I had calmed down the family by this time, and was trying to relax the situation even more by telling them some stories about my previous adventures. Chris and her mother were sitting in front of me listening. (Chris' back was to a wall alongside a doorway which opened into the hall, while her mother was standing right at the doorway. The girl's aunt was sitting next to me on the living room couch.) Then it happened! I was looking right at Chris and her mother when we heard what I can only describe as a noise which sounded like a mild explosion. The sound came directly from the hallway and I dashed to see what had caused it. Right across from the bathroom doorway I found a little plastic compact case. It had apparently flung itself out of the bathroom and had smashed into the hallway wall with such impact as to cause the noise which had so startled us. Yet, oddly, the compact case hadn't even been chipped.

Later that evening, two more objects were thrown. But both incidents occurred when my back was turned on the family members.

The next day was complete with several more ostensible PK displays; and the fact that Chris was the likely—although psychic—source of the outbreak became more evident to us. Even during our first day of investigation we had earmarked Chris as the probable source of the poltergeist. From what we gathered from talking with the older women, nothing odd occurred in the house unless Chris was present, and much of the PK even focused on her. She was undoubtedly the most inquisitive person in the household about the PK, and revealed a peculiar lack of concern about the incidents which were horrifying her relatives. This indicated, at least to me, that this youngster probably knew—even though unconsciously—that she was the source of the outbreak and was probably getting some empathetic enjoyment out of it.

When Chris arose from bed the next morning, Raymond and I knew that the poltergeist would arise as well. Our prediction was accurate: within an hour or so, a loud rap exploded from the kitchen. Neither Raymond nor I were in the kitchen with Chris at the time, so we decided that we would try to keep the family members under our direct surveillance from that time on in order to further authenticate the poltergeist as much as possible. Our plan paid off with multiple dividends. Later that day, as I was sitting with Chris in the living room, we all heard a shrill metallic "ping." I looked up to the hallway and watched a spoon bounce off the opened door and land in the living room. Chris couldn't have thrown it because I was watching her at the time. (Besides, the spoon

Pardon this interruption, but...
if you smoke
and
you're interested
in tar levels
you may find the
information on the back
of this page worthwhile.

A comparison of 57 popular cigarette brands with Kent Golden Lights.

FILTER BRANDS (KING SIZE)

REGULAR	MG TAR	MG NIC	MENTHOL	MG TAR	MG NIC
Kent Golden Lights	8	0.6	**Kent Golden Lights Menthol**	8	0.7
Parliament	10	0.6	Kool Super Lights	9	0.8°
Vantage	11	0.7	Multifilter Menthol	11	0.7
Marlboro Lights	12	0.7	Vantage Menthol	11	0.8
Doral	12	0.8	Salem Lights	11	0.8
Multifilter	12	0.8	Doral Menthol	11	0.8
Winston Lights	12	0.9	Belair	13	1.0°
Raleigh Lights	14	1.0	Marlboro Menthol	14	0.8
Viceroy Extra Milds	14	1.0	Alpine	14	0.8
Viceroy	16	1.0	Kool Milds	14	0.9
Raleigh	16	1.1	Kool	17	1.3
Marlboro	17	1.0	Salem	18	1.2
Tareyton	17	1.2			
Lark	18	1.1			
Pall Mall Filters	18	1.2			
Camel Filters	18	1.2			
L & M	18	1.1			
Winston	19	1.2			

°FTC Method

FILTER BRANDS (100's)

REGULAR	MG TAR	MG NIC	MENTHOL	MG TAR	MG NIC
Kent Golden Lights 100's	10	0.9°	**Kent Golden Lights 100's Menthol**	10	0.9°
Benson & Hedges 100's Lights	11	0.8°	Benson & Hedges 100's Lights Menthol	11	0.8°
Vantage 100's	11	0.9°	Merit 100's Menthol	12	0.9°
Merit 100's	12	0.9°	Virginia Slims 100's Menthol	16	0.9
Parliament 100's	12	0.7	Pall Mall 100's Menthol	16	1.2
Eve 100's	16	1.0	Eve 100's Menthol	16	1.0
Virginia Slims 100's	16	0.9	Silva Thins Menthol	16	1.1
Tareyton 100's	16	1.2	Benson & Hedges 100's Menthol	17	1.0
Marlboro 100's	17	1.0	L & M 100's Menthol	18	1.1
Silva Thins	17	1.3	Kool 100's	18	1.3
Benson & Hedges 100's	17	1.0	Belair 100's	18	1.3
L & M 100's	17	1.1	Winston 100's Menthol	18	1.2
Raleigh 100's	17	1.2	Salem 100's	18	1.3
Viceroy 100's	18	1.3			
Lark 100's	18	1.1			
Pall Mall 100's	19	1.4			
Winston 100's	19	1.3			

°FTC Method

Kings only 8 mg tar

100's only 10 mg tar

Simply put, they're as low as you can go and still get good taste.

Of All Brands Sold: Lowest tar: 0.5 mg. "tar," 0.05 mg. nicotine;
Kent Golden Lights: Kings Regular 8 mg. "tar," 0.6 mg. nicotine.
Kings Menthol 8 mg. "tar," 0.7 mg. nicotine av. per cigarette,
FTC Report August 1977. **100's Regular and Menthol**—10 mg. "tar,"
0.9 mg. nicotine av. per cigarette by FTC Method.

© Lorillard, U.S.A., 1977

bounced *toward* Chris and me, not away from us.) The two older women were in the kitchen with Raymond and couldn't have been responsible either.

Unfortunately, the rest of the day was pure pandemonium. Some friends of the family came to visit in order to watch the "ghost" for themselves and the poltergeist obligingly put on quite a show. But with five people running around the house in fright and excitement, it was hard to keep track of everything that went on. But gradually, by the end of the day, we did discover that by now Chris was helping the poltergeist a bit by throwing an object or two herself. The poltergeist soon abated, and so our investigation came to a close only two days after it had begun.

But what about Chris? What made her into a poltergeist child? And why did she begin to fake? Let me answer these questions in turn.

Chris fits the stereotype of the "poltergeist child" quite well. She was literally aflame with repressed hostilities. To begin with, she had been playing hooky from school and, from what we learned from her mother, it seemed that her classmates had been making fun of her good looks and mature development. Chris herself was overly concerned about her appearance, and wouldn't (or couldn't) face the jeers of her classmates. Her aunt even told me that once she saw her niece look into a mirror and say, "Mirror, I hate you. You make me look ugly." Seconds later, the mirror shattered. So, to us it seemed that Chris was having a hard time coping with her own adolescence and all the frustrations and anxieties this period of life can bring. Secondly, Chris was also having a difficult time coping with her family. She was jealous of her aunt's stay, and her mother's preoccupation with it. She also hated the house in which they lived, and had begged her mother to move. So all in all, Chris was a girl who, at thirteen, was trying to cope with frustrations and guilts which even many an adult would have had a hard time managing. The poltergeist was her means of expressing her despair.

But why did she begin to fake the poltergeistery? Chris is not odd in this respect. Many poltergeist investigators have learned, to their disappointment, that poltergeist children will fake the PK even in cases which are obviously genuine. Several reasons have been proposed for this odd behavior. First of all, children do like to mystify adults and the poltergeist serves as a perfect cover. Also, in many instances, the children will become enamored by all the excitement and attention the poltergeist has generated. So they fake the PK to prolong the poltergeist. It keeps the fun going, so to speak. However, there are also deep underlying psychological reasons why poltergeist children will often resort to trickery. As the genuine PK begins to die down, they may feel an overwhelming urge to express their anger by mimicking the poltergeist's displays. Their behavior may represent an attempt to more openly vent the keyed-up frustrations which have ignited the poltergeist in the first place. They may feel a need to fake, or are actually impelled to fake, in answer to a deeply disturbing and only partially conscious need.

This type of situation developed during an investigation Raymond Bayless and I carried out in 1974 when we were invited down to central Los Angeles to check out a household which had complained to us about some typical poltergeistery. The family had first called the local police substation, and two investigators had been sent out only to return mystified. (The police were playing it very cool, too. When we called the station to confirm the family's story, the police admitted that they had sent out two investigators to look into a "family disturbance." Yet, later that day, they denied any knowledge of the case, even though they had given us the case file number a few hours earlier! The police only urged us *not* to investigate the matter. To say the least, our curiosity was aroused.)

When we arrived at the house that evening, the family told us many stories about the poltergeist's antics. Yet, hardly one hour later, we clearly saw the young daughter of the house throwing things when she thought she could get away with it. Was this case fraudulent through and through? Or was the girl only imitating the poltergeist and faking in answer to some deep-seated need? We will probably never know. However, one parapsychologist friend of mine told me about a poltergeist he once investigated in answer to a news report about the case. He had personally witnessed the disturbances plaguing the victimized home while the teen-age boy, around whom the poltergeist was centering, was right in the room with him. Yet later that day, investigators caught the boy red-handed, faking. He was obviously mimicking the poltergeist.

Over the last two decades, several poltergeist cases have

been investigated both in the United States and in Germany. In the case of Chris and her distressed family, we were only able to surmise that the girl was venting unconscious conflicts and frustrations. We were not able to prove our views, although they were based on self-evident facts, by giving Chris conventional psychological tests. However, on several occasions psychologists and psychiatrists have been able to "diagnose the poltergeist" in just this way. These investigators have almost uniformly discovered that the children are seething with unconscious and unmanageable conflicts and repressed anger.

One of the most active poltergeist hunters in the United States is W. G. Roll, project director for the Durham, North Carolina-based Psychical Research Foundation. Roll has tracked down and confronted several cases since he began his ghost-hunting career in the late 1950s. Today, he boasts of having more first-hand experience in dealing with the poltergeist than any contemporary parapsychologist. He has also had the opportunity not only to witness the poltergeist, but to study several poltergeist children as well.

In 1967, Roll was called in to study a poltergeist which was wreaking havoc in a Miami novelty-store warehouse. Much to the owner's chagrin, objects and novelty items kept falling and flying off the multitiered shelves which lined the storeroom. As Alvin Laubheim, the shop owner, told Roll:

". . . for three days we picked things up off the floor as fast as they could fall down. It was going on all day—quite violently—but not hurting anything, but things would fall to the floor . . . Then finally, delivery men saw these things happening and people coming in and out would see it happen and word got out and there were more and more people coming in."

Laubheim was at his wit's end by the time Roll finally arrived on the scene. But his presence didn't deter the poltergeist either. It gradually became apparent to Roll and his colleagues that the source of the poltergeist's power was a nineteen-year-old Cuban refugee, Julio Vasquez, employed by the warehouse. In fact, the poltergeist seemed most active when Julio was aggravated. As Roll writes in his book, *The Poltergeist:*

"At about two o'clock, an argument developed between Julio and Miss Rambisz. During the weekend, José Diaz, who occasionally worked as medium and was the father of Julio's girlfriend, had gone to the warehouse to see if he could discover whatever was responsible for the events. He said he saw a spirit entity that looked somewhat like an alligator, and he placed various objects, such as fern leaves, in different parts of the room as offerings or 'playthings' for the spirit so that it would stay away from the merchandise. Since nothing had happened either Wednesday or Thursday, the employees were beginning to suspect that this ceremony had been effective. Miss Rambisz wanted the parapsychological investigation to succeed and was telling Julio that the 'voodoo things' should not have been left out since they might be preventing the disturbances. Julio asked, 'Well, who is paying for the breakage?' Miss Rambisz replied, 'That's Al's business.' This discussion was taking place in the north area of the business. Miss Rambisz and Miss Roldan were standing in front of me to my left and Julio was standing at the end of Tier 3 facing us.

"I was looking at Julio, who was just about to reply to Miss Rambisz when the alligator ashtray crashed to the floor behind him. The cowbell remained in place, so the ashtray either must have moved over or around it. I could discover no way in which Julio or anyone else could have produced this event normally. I had Julio and the others under observation and had examined the target area myself. No one had been near it since my last examination."

Since it was clear to Roll and his coinvestigators that Julio was the source of the PK, they hurried him to Durham where psychologists were able to interview him, counsel him, and give him tests. One of these investigators was Dr. Randall Harper, a clinical psychologist who was called on the case in order to evaluate Julio's personality and character. Harper spent considerable time working with Julio and was able to confirm Roll's theory that the poltergeist is a vehicle of expression used by the agent to vent repressed hostility. Harper spent considerable time delving into Julio's fantasies and unexpressed wishes. He concluded about these fantasies in his report, that "the most notable are the many examples of aggressive feelings and impulses which are disturbing and unacceptable to him. He prevents the direct expression of these feelings." He added: "Indeed, he not only controls his expression of aggressive impulses which at base could be sadistic and quite disturbing, but he feels it necessary to even control impulses of a more assertive, as distinct from aggressive, nature."

Randall continued: "There is little self-understanding in relation to these feelings and there may likely be a sense of personal detachment from them. Since they cannot be expressed or acted upon, in any direct way, they are a source of difficulty to him." In other words, Julio was a teen-ager who was trying to cope with anger and aggressions, but crippled by an inability to express these feelings in any normal way. So it would seem that he unconsciously released the poltergeist in order to express these true feelings. He even told Roll—naïvely but revealingly at the same time—that everytime an object was thrown or broken it made him feel happy.

At nineteen, Julio was a little old to be classified as a typical "poltergeist child." Yet, even younger poltergeist children seem to possess the same personality characteristics Julio revealed. They also are beset by problems similar to Julio's, trying to cope with their frustrations and aggression. For example, in 1961 Roll was called to investigate a poltergeist that was disrupting an apartment in Newark, New Jersey, and which focused on a thirteen-year-old boy, Ernie, who was living with his grandmother. Roll brought Ernie back to Durham so the boy could be interviewed by psychologists.

One clinician, who was able to spend considerable time talking with Ernie, reported back to the parapsychologist: "Throughout the three interviews the most striking feature was the degree to which he used denial and repression as defenses. There was considerable evidence of an intense, underlying anger towards his grandmother, but he was never able to verbalize this." Roll had another psychologist examine Ernie. His report confirmed the original diagnosis. After counseling with Ernie, the second psychologist reported back to Roll that "the most striking feature emerging from this examination is his massive use of repression and denial."

W. G. Roll is not the only parapsychologist who has run into these disturbed adolescents during his poltergeist hunts. Dr. John Palmer, then a research associate in the parapsychology division of the University of Virginia's medical school, was called in to investigate a poltergeist in a rural southern town in 1972. As he states in his report, 'A Case of RSPK Involving a Ten-Year-Old-Boy: The Powhatan Poltergeist" (*Journal of the American Society for Psychical*

Research January 1974), this poltergeist delighted in throwing objects about and overturning furniture.

As the events focused on a ten-year-old boy, Dr. Palmer had psychologists interview him in the hope that they could discover the root of the disturbances. One psychologist reported to Palmer: "In coping with aggression, he tends to deny, to avoid, and to withdraw: However, these defenses do not always serve him right and when the external stimulus becomes too strong, anxiety shines through and he can be expected to react in an unpredictable and irresponsible manner."

What, then, is the poltergeist telling us about our children and their psychic potentials? To begin with, the poltergeist does alert us to the fact that each of our children might possess considerable psychic talent. The power behind the poltergeist is no mean force! Yet, *how* our children will eventually use their psychic potentials will probably result from the way they are brought up. All the children discussed in this report were plagued by a total inability to express frustration, hostility and anger normally. These children weren't born with this psychological disability. Somehow, as they grew up, they *learned* not to express hostility even in generally acceptable ways, out of fear of rejection or reprisal.

Perhaps there is a message here. Young parents, if they are interested in their children's psychic development, should permit them to express their feelings—both good and bad—openly, in a conventional manner, and without fear. The poltergeist is just as much our responsibility as it is anybody else's. Every parent who is aware of the human potential movement knows that his child can potentially become a psychic, sage, or mystic. However, there is a seedier side to the picture as well. If a child grows up in a family which expresses love and anger in a normal and healthy fashion, no doubt the child will learn to express his psychic potential in a similarly healthy fashion. But if he grows up in a family in which the members cannot air their feelings and needs, the child's psychic abilities might turn on his family and himself. And they will release that most amazing of all spectacles . . . the poltergeist.

9. "I am Begotten by a Demon . . ."

Harald Bonwick, Jr.

England's demon children are an integral part of British religious history and folklore. Yet the realities or myths of their existence throw their shadow upon our own age. Even a prominent twentieth-century figure, Aleister Crowley, encouraged the rumor that he had been spawned by a union between a demon and his pious, god-fearing mother. Mr. Bonwick, after studying at Harvard and Duke universities, has lectured on "Roots of Western Occultism" on the European continent and at institutes of higher learning in the Middle East; he describes his interests as "narrowing down on the area where empirical parapsychology, religion and anthropology must eventually find a common ground."

Towards the beginning of this century, the Catholic publishing firm of Burns & Oates in London published *Amphora*, a book of devotional hymns to the Virgin Mary. Both lay and Catholic reviewers were enthusiastic; the *Catholic Herald* spoke of it as "page after page of most exquisite praise of Her." The book was a sensation.

Amphora was published anonymously, but it was soon rumored in literary circles that a famous stage actress accepted credit for writing it. At that, the real poet revealed his identity with a demonic laugh and leer: he was none other than the man who originated such diabolical rites of sex magic that even the most sensational papers of Fleet Street were timorous in describing them. Many works of elaborate and blasphemous pornography under his own name were never even allowed to be reviewed in family newspapers.

The man's name was Aleister Crowley, and he capped his

joke upon the Church by pointing out that in each of the *Amphora* poems, the name of Hecate, Lilith, Isis, or Ashtoreth could be substituted for the name Mary. Crowley's action, while typical of him, was not entirely of this world. His own mother, a pious and god-fearing woman, had stated that he was the Great Beast of the Apocalypse incarnate. One can imagine her lonely shuddering at the thought that she had unwittingly born the spawn of an incubus. It is not easy to contemplate her feelings upon learning that he mocked her by taking the name of the Great Beast 666 as his own for the rest of his demonic career.

Today, the world is so full of confidence in its specious knowledge that it can magnanimously *understand* anything in terms of materialistic concepts. It is inclined to write off the legend of the "demon child" in terms of a secondary personality or as a case of possession. This attitude, intended to reflect the enlightenment of our times, neglects much valid evidence that we have from history's pages. For there were times in which the unusual behavior of a child was not dismissed in terms of pseudopsychiatric cant or overlooked in the name of materiality. These records are the work of sincere men, quite knowledgable for their days, who took pains to put down on paper the things they saw and could not understand. If we put aside the idea that Science must always be right, we find that those historical testimonies tell us stories of children who were definitely not of this world. We must remember that Science-which-is-always-right, the practical science of the nineteenth century, has already been replaced to a great extent by such disciplines as quantum field theory and transpersonal psychology, two legitimate fields of research that may, by comparison, be more "far out," say, than any question of demon children.

Traditionally, the demon child was begot by an incubus who lay with a married woman. Often times, to effect his diabolic congress, the demon would assume the form, or appearance of the woman's husband. It was believed that intercourse with a married woman was chosen because it was particularly offensive to God, due to the added element of adultery. It was conceivable, then, that a woman might bear a demon's child and not be aware of it—unless, as sometimes happened, the secret were told to torment her.

Sexual intercourse at witches sabbaths were notoriously sterile, except when they involved a thoroughly human partner. The demon child had no soul. Church fathers taught that the semen conveyed only the physical attributes of the person and that the soul was added by the Divinity, something that would never be allowed to occur in the case of demon offspring.

One can see, then, the possibility that Aleister Crowley was sired by an incubus upon a woman who thought she embraced her husband. The element of soullessness would certainly account for the satanic sadism of his sense of humor. Naturally, Crowley has otherwise been explained in terms of the various schools of psychology; but one must admit that he can also be explained in an older, nonmaterialistic tradition as well.

Let's look at some of the earliest recorded cases of demon children.

Gervase of Tilbury was a monk of Christ Church in Canterbury. He recorded the tale of a demon boy who appeared in the vaults below the monastery of Prüm at Trier in the Rhineland. This was in 1138, and the story was well known in other monasteries throughout Europe.

Now, in the Abbey of Prüm the wine stock was kept down in the dark and forbidding vaults, many meters below the ground. One day, when the cellarer and his assistant went to the wine cellar to draw wine for the communion service, they found that a cask that should have been full was emptied right down to its bunghole. This worried the cellarer who felt that, if the abbot heard about it, he would lose his job. With that in mind, he went to the cellar again in the evening and made sure that all the wine kegs were securely bunged.

But the next morning, inspection revealed that another of the casks was half empty. He repeated his security procedures of the previous night, but to no avail. On the third morning, a third keg was found to have been tapped. The cellarer went to the abbot and related his strange tale. The abbot pondered the problem and, realizing that no human agency could have got past the locked door to the cellar, ordered that the bungs of all wine kegs should be annointed with holy oil.

At dawn the next day, the cellarer and his assistant found a young boy, with his hands stuck fast to one of the bungs. They tore him loose, and with much struggling, took him to the abbot who questioned him, particularly as to how he had managed to get into the locked and guarded cellar. The boy either could not or would not speak, but conducted himself as a mute. The abbot ordered that the boy be dressed in a monk's robe and be allowed to live with the younger scholars at the monastery. Though he did, he never spoke, ate, or slept. He spent all night seated upon his bed, constantly sighing or moaning in a most piteous way.

After a time, the abbot of another monastery came to visit. As he sat with the head of Prüm monastery, he saw the scholars passing back and forth in the cloisters in silent meditation. But, as the boy passed, he held out his hand to the visiting abbot as if in supplication.

The visitor asked why such a young boy was in the monastery and was told the tale of the raided cellar. He was visibly upset. "Get rid of him, right away!" he shouted. "That's no boy; that's a demon! If it hadn't been for the holy relics you have here, he'd have done you all kinds of injury!" The boy was brought to the abbot who began to strip him of the monk's garment he wore—but in his very hands he vanished like smoke!

The mission of a demon is to break down the order of society in order to discredit the Divinity in favor of the Master he serves. He likes to discredit holy people and holy traditions. Aleister Crowley's mother, as devout a member of the Plymouth Brethren as she was, would have been a prime target of attention for a demon who chose to impose upon her in the guise of her husband.

Gervase of Tilbury chronicled the tale of the boy in the vault in his *Otia Imperialia* which he wrote for Emperor Otto IV of Germany. Scholars consider the work to give an authentic picture of the times. Shortly we'll look at another of his accounts. Right now, let's examine the case of a young boy who turned up in Pembrokeshire, West Wales, a few years after the Prüm incident. It happened in the house of a knight, Eliodorus de Stackpol. His stone effigy is still to be seen in Stackpol Church in Pembrokeshire.

A young boy, a stranger, was earning his keep by making himself generally useful around the Stackpol house. He was called Simon. It was soon noticed that any errand assigned him, no matter how difficult or time-consuming, was performed perfectly and at once.

Then it was noticed that errands were often performed before anyone spoke to him about them. He was obviously reading the minds of the people in the house! Naturally, he was questioned about this ability and what he said caused Stackpol and his lady a severe shock: he knew all their personal secrets, even where they hid their gold and jewels. He could describe everything the Stackpols had concealed from all but themselves. Lord and lady brought the questioning session to an abrupt end.

The boy never slept in the house; no one knew where he did sleep; but he was always on hand to report the completion of their unspoken orders. The Stackpol children took to spying on him. They noticed his habit, when he thought he was unobserved, of kneeling over a still mill dam and speaking down into it in a strange tongue, as if in conversation with something in its depths. The children ran and told their parents.

The Stackpols called the boy to them and sacked him. Lady Stackpol asked, "Who art thou?"

He said: "I am begotten by a Demon upon the wife of a yokel of this parish. He lay upon her in the shape of her own husband." He named the woman, whose husband was then dead, and she confessed to them that she knew the boy was a demon child. The account was recorded by Giraldus Cambrensis, a very respected ecclesiastical scholar of the late twelfth and early thirteenth centuries, in his *Itineraria Cambriae*.

One may wonder that the boy seems only to have done good for the Stackpols, but we must remember that he never slept in the house at night and thus we have no knowledge of what he did during the dark hours. He may have used the Stackpols' home as a cover for his darker operations, ingratiating himself with them so that he would have someplace to shelter and eat—for a demon child needs food just as vitally as does a human one.

One remarkable thing upon which most medieval chroniclers and church authorities agree is that very frequently the demon child is spirited away from its earthly mother. This usually occurs a few days or weeks after birth. Those that remain often run away at about age seven. Though at birth they are puny, relative to normal children, they weigh more than a child should. Later they outstrip normal children in size and a prodigious strength. Crowley was a big man and powerfully athletic.

An extraordinary tale of two such children who seem to have been spirited away, and then quite accidentally returned, is told by Gervase of Tilbury, in his *Otia* and by his contemporary, Abbot Ralph of Coggeshall, in his *Chronica Anglicarum*. It was also noted by William of Newburgh, in his *Historia Rerum Anglicarum.*

In 1184, at a place now called Woolpits (near Bury St. Edmunds), but then known as St. Mary de Wulfpetes, there was a deep chasm with holes in its walls where wolves made their lairs. One day, field workers found two children scrabbling over the rocks in manifest panic and weeping inconsolably. Their skins were bright green!

The workers took the children to the house of Sir Richard de Calne at Wikes, not far away. Food was put before them, but they would not touch it, though they were quite apparently hungry. Nor could anyone understand their language. Finally, someone tore some beans from a stalk and handed them to the green children. The beans they recognized and gobbled down with delight. For a long time they lived on beans alone, touching no other food. The boy, the younger of the two, gradually sickened and died. The girl's skin, particularly after she was coaxed onto a normal diet, grew paler until she assumed a normal beige color. She eventually learned English.

The girl's story was that she and her brother had lived in a strange land with their father. No sun shone in that land. There was neither sunrise nor sunset, only a condition like our dusk. Far from them, across a great river, they could see a beautiful land, brightly illuminated, but no one could cross the river to reach it.

One day, while guarding some small animals of their father, they began to explore a cave. Led on by a sound like church bells, they came out of the cave into the wolf pit. After wandering around a while, they lost the location of their own cave and began to panic. It was then that the laborers came upon them.

The narrow cave and the sound of bells, the twilight land and the stream that could not be crossed, will be familiar to modern readers familiar with experiences of people who have "died" in hospitals, but were resuscitated. The green children appear to have gone through that process in reverse, arriving in our world from that land seen by the resuscitated who had been clinically dead.

Many religious traditions treat of a Limbo, a space where there is no reward or punishment, but only existence. Traditionally, those who are soulless go there when they die, forever separated from higher planes by a natural barrier. If the demon child is a soulless child, spirited from its mother, that is where it would end up.

"We come from St. Martin's Land," said the girl. She would have known of no St. Martin, but "St. Martin's Land" was a Christian euphemism for "Malkin's Land," a region of "grammarye and necromancy" and of demons in early European tradition. It was variously—and quite erroneously—located at the Antipodes or deep under the earth. The most economical analysis of the facts in the case suggests that the green children were two demon offspring who accidentally stumbled back into this life again.

The girl worked for a while at Sir Richard de Calne's as a domestic. She was said to have been *nimium lasciva* and *petulans exstitit* (wanton and lascivious) by Coggeshall. Newburgh said she married a man King's Lynn in Norfolk and lived happily ever after.

10. The Many Lives of Doris Fischer

Thomas R. Tietze

The case of the girl known as Doris Fischer is, by all odds, the most absorbing, best documented, and essentially most tragic in the annals of modern psychical research. Mr. Tietze is particularly well qualified to present the dramatic story of Doris' multiple personalities, as he has made a special study of the young woman's mentor, one of the leading researchers in his field; his notable paper, "Ursa Major: An Impressionistic Appreciation of Walter Franklin Prince," appeared in the Journal *of the American Society for Psychical Research (January 1976). Thomas R. Tietze, who teaches in Minneapolis, is the author of* Margery, *a biography of the controversial Boston medium Mina S. Crandon.*

When the girl first came to Dr. Prince's office in 1910, there were many still alive who would have attributed her case to demonic possession. Psychologists had really very little knowledge of the curious phenomena associated today with the term "Multiple Personality." Literally, only a handful of cases had by that time been reported, and in all instances the interpretation of several distinct personalities inhabiting one body had been ridiculed as naïve by respected psychologists.

Nevertheless, it was a most appropriate choice young "Doris Fischer" (as she would later become known) made when she approached Walter Franklin Prince for help. One of the few people in America who had surveyed the literature of multiple personality, Prince was at that time heading a counseling office for All Saints' Church in Pittsburgh. At the church's rector, he had long been interested in psychotherapy for troubled parishoners and would retain that interest for the next several years.

Doris' case impressed Prince immediately as a peculiarly complex mental disturbance. Initially, he had supposed that the girl was exhibiting symptoms of "hysteria." But instead of the expected behavior of the emotionally ill hysteric, Prince noted that Doris responded differently each time he presented her with a stimulus. For instance, at one session he gave her food that she ate with apparent delight; yet, at the next session she asserted that she hated the very same food. Occasionally, when he talked to her, Doris assumed radically different facial expressions: a stolid, dull, and uninterested Doris would, when Prince next looked up at her, suddenly have a keen glint in her eye and a mischievous smile on her lips. Sometimes, in excited tones, the twenty-one-year-old girl expressed an enthusiasm for colored pictures, similar to that of a high-spirited infant; at other times, she merely gazed, in an unfocused way, in the general direction of the very same pictures.

Prince decided that these behavior patterns pointed to dissociation of personality, and he began to treat Doris practically full-time. In order to do so, he had to find out what Doris' childhood had been like. The picture that emerged from his investigation was a true-life horror story, all the more frightening because, though the results were unexpected, the causes are even today all too common.

Born in 1889, Doris experienced infancy in tragic circumstances. Her mother, a sadly victimized wife of a vicious alcoholic, was compelled, for economic reasons, to turn the care of Doris over to Helen, one of her many children. Doris' father was rarely at home. Her mother was usually out in the neighborhood doing cleaning, washing, and other odd jobs she could turn up. Helen was no substitute for her parents; and, despite the love Mrs. Fischer clearly felt for Doris, the circumstances inevitably led to her daughter's breakdown. Remote from her older siblings, a quiet and withdrawn child, Doris turned inward for the exercise of her imagination and for the affection she failed to find in her external environment. When she was three years old, crises occurred that resulted in one of the most bizarre case studies in the annals of abnormal psychology.

One night in 1892, Doris' father came home. Seeing his wife about to place Doris in their bed, he flew into a petulant, drunken rage. Tearing the child from the woman's hands, he threw Doris fiercely to the floor. With a shriek, Mrs. Fischer swept her daughter into her arms and ran to Helen's room. Doris was not crying, so Mrs. Fischer placed her in the absent sister's bed and returned to confront her husband.

It was then, as Doris lay alone in bed, that Margaret first came. Doris was by then crying, and her sisters on the same floor yelled to her to "Shut up" No one was there to comfort her, so someone came "out" from the inside.

In the years that followed, the secondary personality, Margaret, became a fully developed "other" girl. She was rarely around when Doris was awake, but did leave evidence of her existence that, as the baby became a girl, puzzled and alarmed both Doris and her mother. Occasionally, Mrs. Fischer would see Doris apparently having a conversation— even a quarrel—with herself. When Doris began her schooling, Margaret, too, learned to write; from that point on, Margaret formed the habit of leaving notes for Doris. These were sometimes consoling, sometimes threatening, and sometimes embarrassing. Like any two young girls, their moods would be expressed at times by affection and at times by hostility. The difference, of course, was that the two girls lived in one body.

An early childhood experience impressed Doris with Margaret's independence and even sovereignty. Margaret had her own toys, which were not to be touched by Doris. Once Doris picked up a ball belonging to Margaret. Suddenly, impelled by an apparently external will, her left hand reached up and "plowed scratches in her cheeks and eyelids until they bled." From ages four to eight, Doris' face usually bore evidence of Margaret's vigilence and discipline. Afterwards, it was only when Doris forgot her early lessons that Margaret felt it necessary to scratch Doris' face.

When Doris was at school, Margaret might without warning, as she put it, "come out." During these periods of Margaret's emergence, she would play pranks and indulge in displays of temperament foreign to the normally serious Doris. Then, rascal that she was, she would leave Doris to take the punishment for deeds of which she was entirely unaware.

Discipline was hard for Doris, since Margaret was frequently "coming out" in order to rush from the classroom when lessons were dull or the room hot. When she returned, she would be giggling, or, occasionally, soaked to the skin, having taken a dip in a nearby stream. Whimsical, witty, and even charmingly roguish, Margaret was both the bane and delight of Doris' teachers, although they, too, were puzzled by the child's rapid alterations of personality. For a few years, Margaret insisted on calling herself "Luella"—despite Doris' distaste for the name—and Doris' report cards frequently refer to her as Luella. When she was in control, Doris would apologize for her misdeeds, even though she knew little or nothing of what had happened while Margaret was "out." Both Doris and Margaret learned their lessons, until two years before the end of her schooling. Then, the material became too advanced for Margaret's limited intellect, so she stopped sharing responsibility for homework, and Doris went on alone. Despite all the marks against her conduct, Doris received grades that allowed her to pass on to high school.

But there Margaret balked. She had had enough of school. Instead, she permitted Doris to continue the more interesting jobs which she had, because of her father's financial straits, taken up from the age of seven.

At home, Margaret tried to keep her existence a secret, as she later confessed to Dr. Prince. To the mother, however, there was no clue that would convince her that she had on her hands anything more puzzling than "a bundle of contradictory moods, incomprehensible at times, but lovable always." Her approach to discipline was remarkably "advanced" in those pre-Dr. Spock days. Instead of punishing her daughter for her odd behavior, Mrs. Fischer instinctively resorted to strategy and to affection, reinforcing the "normal" personality.

Doris and her mother continued to grow closer. Her fantasies of a happy future were encouraged by her mother as they worked together at the wash. To Doris, this wishful thinking was both helpful and debilitating; fantasies and exercises of imagination, for a mind so delicately balanced, contributed to Doris' inability to hold tightly to reality. The mother was Doris' closest friend, beloved confidante, and model for the stability of personality.

On May 5, 1906, Mrs. Fischer lay down, suddenly ill, with no one to help her. Her husband was home, but had once again drunk himself into a condition in which he could not

have helped anyone. Doris, impelled by an odd, perhaps telepathic, feeling, had come home early that day. Nothing could
be done, however. By two o'clock the following morning,
Mrs. Fischer was dead.

A pain shot through the left side of Doris' head as she realized that her mother was dead. She withdrew from consciousness, and another dissociation, or splitting personality,
occurred. This tragic incident marked the first appearance of
the splinter self that came to be called "Sick Doris." Without
a memory, without a language, without a recognition of
people, places, or objects, Sick Doris appeared when Doris
was seventeen years old. She was, to all outward appearances,
little more than an infant.

Her face was expressionless and flabby (no doubt from the
relaxation of her facial muscles), and her eyes were shifty
and dull, without a hint of the mirth and mischief of Margaret or the openness of Doris. As Dr. Prince later put it, "All
affection was gone, and all grief; not a tremor remained of
the mental agony of a few moments before. She was as one
born with an adult body, and a maturely inquiring mind, but
with absolutely no memory and absolutely no knowledge."

As the months following her first awakening drew on, Sick
Doris learned to speak and comprehend with great rapidity.
She was also able to do work requiring manual dexterity, actually much better than either Doris or Margaret. Her em-
broidering work, Prince reported, "was exquisite," while the
other two personalities tended to be clumsy, unimaginative,
and impatient with the task.

The disturbances deepened the following year when Doris
suffered a bad fall and injured her neck and back. A fragment of another self emerged at that time which Margaret
named "Sleeping Real Doris." Appearing only when Doris
was asleep, this odd splinter had only a recognizable facial
expression—"one of quizzical puzzlement," Dr. Prince
says—and she spoke with a "characteristic harsh, croaking"
voice. She appeared to have memories of her own, unshared
by the Doris or Margaret personalities. Quite often, she was
little more than a kind of tape recorder, repeating one side of
conversations in which Doris had participated from childhood
on, up to the day before. However, Dr. Prince thought it
doubtful that Sleeping Doris had any knowledge of her own
existence, though he did suspect that she had the intellectual
potential to learn and grow.

During these bizarre years, Doris was neither a full personality herself nor a mere house in which the other selves dwelt. She was a seriously disturbed young woman who had been able—just barely—to hold her sanity together sufficiently to make a solitary living.

When she appeared in Prince's office, the secondary personalities endeavored to remain hidden, but it was not long before Prince had the general outlines of the case sketched in his mind. Before his study of Doris' dissociation was over, he had uncovered all four of the personalities and had made the acquaintance of yet one more. His treatment, lasting more than three years, was necessarily highly experimental but nonetheless cautious. Prince was no casual analyst asking for an hour a week; he invited Doris to come and live with him and his wife. As the treatment continued, Doris became so much a part of the life of the childless couple that, in 1912, they adopted her.

After much badgering and cajoling, Margaret confessed her existence, and Prince came to know and even love her peculiar traits. She was not, he thought, a splinter being like the others. She had her own tastes, her own expressions and gestures, her own tone of voice, all clearly differentiated from Doris. There was much in the impish, excitable, irresponsible Margaret that would have been healthy characteristics for Doris to acquire, but Prince recognized that, for Doris to be cured, Margaret must disappear.

Day after day, Prince worked tirelessly in his effort to rescue Doris' mental health. In a tribute to Prince's work by one of America's most distinguished psychologists, Dr. Gardner Murphy, the author states that Prince "was going to put together the parts by driving out some and by interweaving . . . others. He was going to resynthesize the shattered personality by emphasizing the laws of dissociation and reassociation." Many of these "laws" he would have to discover himself.

Sick Doris was the first fragment to deal with. Less like an individual and more like a cloud hovering over Doris, her unexpected appearance threatened at any time to cast Doris into unhappiness and despondancy, a kind of emotionless Limbo. Sick Doris' main pleasure in her bizarre "life" was to work at embroidery and sewing. In order to discourage her "coming out," Prince made her life annoying for her, primarily by keeping Sick Doris' sewing things out of her reach.

It was painful to watch the blank, childish face twist into expressions of confusion and frustration. It was wrenching for Prince to hold the baby Sick Doris in his arms as she withdrew from that distortion of life that had been all she knew, but he had to do it. After months of association with these personalities, they had come to hold a place in his heart—had become a kind of one-person family. But his job was clear. Sick Doris gradually "died."

Through hypnotic suggestion, Prince continued to work on the other two selves. The vague and undeveloped Sleeping Doris was easier to dislodge and erase than was the vivacious Margaret.

Margaret herself claimed to be an utterly independent being who watched Doris' every activity. Prince's habit was to treat such assertions at face value and deal with Margaret on the level she created for herself. Meanwhile, Prince continued his hypnotic attacks on Margaret's supremacy. As Murphy writes, "Day by day, month by month, the girl with the mental habits of a ten-year-old went back through nine, eight, and so on until she talked baby talk, looked with a child's glance, and finally lapsed into the emptiness of social comprehension that appears in the newborn."

During one such hypnotic session, Prince became aware, for the first time, of yet another fragment of Doris' consciousness. Here is Prince's dramatic account of that encounter:

"In the evening she came in looking very jaded and miserable, and was evidently suffering. She said little, but it is nearly certain that Margaret had been punishing her for coming to the rectory in the afternoon in spite of the subliminal urgings to stay away, and that she dared not tell what she had gone through for fear of further torments. Presently she lay down and went to sleep. Margaret came, and clutched savagely at the left hip. . . , and scratched the neck. I remonstrated in vain. . . . Attempting suggestion I began to say impressively, 'I am going to take away your power. You are growing weaker. You are losing your strength.' The struggles became weaker. Finally I said, 'Your strength is gone. You are powerless.'

"All striving ceased, the face changed, and she awoke. She now appeared extremely languid, and spoke with difficulty, but said that she felt no pain. Her vital forces seemed to be ebbing away, and she gradually passed into a condition which made Mrs. Prince and me think . . . that she was dying.

"Her pulse descended to 54, and became feeble. She seemed only half conscious, but occasionally looked wonderingly at the two who were sitting by her. . . . At length she murmured, 'Am I dying?'

" 'I think so.'

" 'Don't you want me to go?' She smiled peacefully, as though glad both to go and to know that she was to be missed. . . .

"Under the spell of considerable emotion I was looking into her eyes, and presently her gaze fixed upon mine, and with parted lips she continued to look, not rigidly, but dreamily and peacefully, while we waited for the end which we thought so near. After some time it suddenly struck me that her gaze and features were unnaturally fixed—I stooped to examine her.

"Just then a voice issued from her lips, though no other feature moved: 'You must get her out of this. She is in danger.'

"It was as startling as lightning from the blue sky. . . . There was a calm authority in her tone which was new. I shook the girl gently; her face did not change.

" 'Shake her harder,' the voice went on. 'Hurry! Hurry!'

"It was evident that Doris was in a profound state of hypnosis, and I began vigorous measures to bring her out. . . .

" 'Walk her! Walk her!' said the voice.

"At first there was difficulty in carrying out this order, [since] she stumbled and tended to collapse upon the carpet. Directions occasionally continued to issue from the lips, directions which I supposed to be uttered by Margaret suddenly most singularly endowed with wisdom and calmness, directions which I never thought of disregarding, they were delivered with such authority and characterized by such good sense.

"Finally we heard, 'She is coming to herself now; she will be all right soon.'

"No more directions were given, and almost at once the face showed more animation and intelligence."

This was the first appearance of Sleeping Margaret, a fascinating creature with wit, warmth, intelligence, and even wisdom, who claimed to be Doris's "spirit guard." It was her job, she claimed, to watch over and protect Doris from harm. She had been with Doris and conscious ever since the first dissociating shock. Sleeping Margaret became Prince's foremost ally in his struggle with Margaret.

Although Margaret was a pleasant, if alarmingly mischievous, little girl, she was far from being a guardian angel. On one occasion, Dr. Prince advised Doris to pray for relief from the hearing of voices all about her.

"Remember that Jesus helped people who had troubles. Perhaps if you pray the voices will leave," Prince suggested.

Immediately, he noticed her body writhe as though in pain caused by Margaret's subliminal exertions.

"Directly her eyes closed," Prince reported, "her face underwent that strange transformation, and a sharp voice cried, 'What made you tell Doris to pray? I don't want her to pray!'

" 'Why don't you want her to? Do you dread prayer?'

" 'Yes.'

"Here I uttered a prayer aloud. At once the life went out of the hands, and they sank upon her breast. The head rolled over to one side, and her lips parted in quiet slumber."

Sleeping Margaret, as she later listened to this part of the transcript, said that at this point, "Margaret went away."

Hypnosis, prayer, constant attention, and complete personal devotion were the tools Prince utilized to rid Doris of Margaret. When at last Margaret disappeared, never to return, Prince felt a genuine sadness. After Prince's death in 1934, a friend revealed that "the toys which had been Margaret's were kept by Dr. Prince in a special drawer all the rest of his life, exactly like the possessions of a little girl who has been lost."

But once Margaret had been exorcised, what remained to be said about her essential nature? Was she what she claimed to be—a possessing entity? Or was she a psychological fragment of Doris? Again to quote Dr. Murphy: "There is nothing in the published material which forces us to believe that Margaret was a spirit. Neither is there anything to prove that she was just an 'aspect' of Doris—or any more dependent upon her than Michelangelo's personality was on Raphael's. They were two *persons* in relation to the same organism. This is obscure, psychologically baffling; but the record is there and has not been refuted."

In 1913, with the cure of Doris' dissociation and the restoration of her physical health, one of the several secondary personalities remained. How can Prince have pronounced Doris cured when two persons still inhabited her body?

The diagnosis was by no means an easy one for Prince to reach. On the one hand, it did not seem healthy for a young woman to talk in her sleep, proclaim herself in the course of these conversations to be a spirit, and then stoutly refuse to respond to the kind of treatment Prince had used in dealing with Margaret, Sick Doris, and other splinter selves that had developed along the long road to mental stability.

But on the other hand, Sleeping Margaret had been a very positive curative influence. It had been she who had instructed Prince to attempt certain therapeutic methods, and it had been she who had rescued Doris, time and again, from the childish depredations of the often vicious Margaret. Moreover, in Doris' later life, Sleeping Margaret proved invaluable many times, warning Doris in advance against ill-advised actions.

In short, Sleeping Margaret seemed to be a kind of reliable, cool, common-sense version of the normal Doris. In 1926 Prince published an account of psychical phenomena, seemingly caused by Sleeping Margaret, entitled *Psychic in the House*. Doris' own psychical abilities seem to have been channeled through her dream self, Sleeping Margaret, as though Doris were a medium and Sleeping Margaret her "control"—her contact with the spiritual world. Indeed, in the early 1920s, Una, Lady Troubridge, in a penetrating analysis of mediumistic "spirit controls" published by the Society of Psychical Research, London, pointed out many striking similarities between the Margaret personality and "Feda," the famous spirit control of Mrs. Gladys Osborne Leonard, the British medium.

It is, however, the opinion of many modern parapsychologists that despite Sleeping Margaret's ostensible psychic capacities—and Margaret's, which had cropped up now and again during the period of dissociation—there is no necessity to suppose that either Sleeping Margaret or Margaret were spirits. Modern research has established that ESP need no longer be regarded as the exclusive property of ghosts; perfectly ordinary people have psychic capacities, with no question of spirit intervention.

From the time of her recovery, Doris led a perfectly wholesome and happy life as the Princes' adopted daughter. Few who knew them failed to be touched by the utter devo-

tion of therapist and patient—now become father and child.
The death, in 1925, of Mrs. Lelia Prince was a serious loss to
Doris, but it was the death of Prince in 1934 that dealt her a
staggering blow.

In spite of the most devoted care by all of her friends, notably Prince's colleague, the Reverend Elwood Worcester,
Doris retreated into total loneliness and despair. At least one
suicide attempt, through the swallowing of pellets of strychnia
and morphia, was averted by the quick action of a hospital
team. But tortured visions of inimical spirits and horrible
nightmares continued to plague her. Although Worcester was
hopeful of Doris' recovery in 1935, in the end the woman
died, insane, in a sanatorium. Thus ended one of the most
dramatic, tragic, and significant stories to be found in the
literature of psychology and psychical research, at the common root of both disciplines: the enigma of the human personality.

11. Murder of the Child Witch

Paul Langdon

Bernadette confessed defiantly that she was wedded to the devil. According to one authority, she had been abandoned "by all human sentiment" and died alone in the night, "without any hope of divine aid, an expectation that had long been destroyed within her very soul." The girl's confessors had become her torturers, and finally her killers. Mr. Langdon studied court records, interviewed religious authorities and psychologists to compile this unique account.

The year was 1969, not 1596. The town was a citadel of modern civilization, not a medieval village. But a group had banded together to beat, and beat again, and to torture a bewildered, brainwashed young woman accused of witchcraft—until she died; and they now stood trial for the killing.

It took almost three years for the trial preparations at Zurich, Switzerland. She had died on May 14, 1966. Her name was Bernadette Hasler; she was 17 years old. The Hasler parents had turned their little girl over to the practitioners of a "Holy Family." This weird cult was directed by a defrocked and excommunicated South German priest, 61-year-old Josef Stocker, and his mistress, 54-year-old Magdalena Kohler.

The fate of Bernadette was merely the most extreme example of the religious fanaticism that held the cult together in a boiling cauldron of emotion. Their original "inspiration" had come from an obscure Carmelite nun, one Sister Stella, who claimed a "direct telephone to heaven." However, the Stocker-Kohler team found not only an outlet for its religiously-oriented sexual sadism within the cult, but also a means for demanding money and luxuries from its followers. The cult, with headquarters outside Zurich, had begun with the visions of the nun Stella in about 1959 in the German town of Singen in the Black Forest.

The nun, known as "Little Star" to her followers, had told Stocker and Kohler that they had been chosen to lead the survivors through a future Apocalypse. The couple later convinced their followers to stock the headquarters of the "Holy Family" with sacks of flour, sugar, hundreds of cans of food, and even a cow boarded with a nearby farmer.

Forced to flee Germany, Stocker and Kohler spent seven years on the Hasler farm, in hiding. Little Bernadette Hasler then lived a slave's existence, while being mentally and physically persecuted, largely by Magdalena Kohler. Over and over again, for months on end, the young girl was bullied into "confessing" her alleged dealings with the devil, her impure thoughts, her wicked desires. (The Haslers, over the years, spent 200,000 Swiss francs—U.S. $46,000.00—on the two cult leaders.)

The type of religio-sexual confessions Stocker and Kohler forced from their followers is illustrated by the statistics in one written account: "I have taken communion improperly, 6,000 times; I have prayed wrongly 450 times; I have given 750 tongue kisses; 1,000 times have I undertaken the sexual act in my imagination."

Bernadette was forced by Mrs. Kohler to write detailed confessions covering 330 pages. The pathetic statements of the young girl reflected the sexual suggestions of her "Mother Confessor," rather than her own naïve imagination. She wrote, for instance, "I love the Devil. He is beautiful. He visits me nearly every night. He is much better than God. I would like to belong only to the Devil."

Such "confessions" then prompted Stocker, Kohler, and four members of their cult to beat the young girl with horsewhips and canes, "to drive the Devil out of her." According to one psychiatric authority during the Zurich trial, Professor Hans Binder, Bernadette had been driven into a veritable "sin mania," perhaps unable to differentiate between reality and the hallucinatory existence created by Stocker and Kohler. The psychiatrist noted that the cheerful child, given to fun and laughter, had turned into "a depressed creature," who saw her life as "a chain of sins."

As punishment for her "sinful life," the girl was not permitted to go for walks, had to give up her violin lessons and was not allowed to talk with other children. Her "Holy Parents" abused her with such epithets as "Satan's Mate" and "Devil's Whore." The Kohler woman (whose relationship with Stocker was supposed to be merely "spiritual," but who had given birth to a child) called Bernadette a "perverted piece" and a "lying swine."

But when Magdalena Kohler was asked, during the trial, whether she disliked Bernadette, she answered, "No." And when the president of the court asked why, then, she had cursed the girl, the answer was, "I merely loved the girl. I only cursed her because she had a pact with the Devil."

According to Dr. Binder's psychiatric findings, Magdalena had created such a world of delusion that she was "sincerely convinced she was only doing what God demanded. She had no idea that it was, in reality, her own unconscious, primitive self that prompted her gruesome actions against Bernadette." The emotional breaking point for the girl came, apparently, when Kohler refused Easter confession for her, one month before she was beaten to death. It was at this point, according to the psychiatric analysis, that Bernadette crossed the border into a hysteria of being possessed by the devil. It was then, in defiance of Stocker and Kohler and the God they allegedly represented, that Bernadette insisted on having a "pact with Satan." Having been refused the support of God, she turned to the devil for a Satanic counterpower. This, Professor Binder said, while obviously irrational, was the "logic of a defiant heart."

The charismatic power of Magdalena Kohler over members of the cult was illustrated, during the court hearings, by the case of one of her followers, 37-year-old Paul Barmettler. She had forbidden him to have sexual intercourse with his wife, and he complied. Together with his brothers, 46-year-old Hans and 41-year-old Heinrich, Barmettler participated in the maltreatment of Bernadette that led to her death. A fourth cultist and torture participant was Emilio Bettio.

Barmettler paid the "Holy Family" 10 per cent of his income, took over the mortgage payments on the chalet in Ringwil, near Zurich, and—because of a "holy message"—abandoned his hunting hobby. His brother Hans, a railroad official with a modest income and the father of five, also made monthly payments to Stocker-Kohler and contributed to the purchase of a handsome car, a Mercedes 300. The

third brother, Heinrich, also a railroad worker, broke an en-
gagement at the behest of Magdalena. He remains a bache-
lor.

The sexual control which Magdalena exercised over these
men was counterbalanced in Bernadette's confessions. Her
statements contained a description of her "marriage to Lucifer," head devil: "I wore a white dress and he had his black,
shiny fur. It was a beautiful picture." The confessions also
contained the passage that after the death of her "Holy
Parents," she planned to marry 10 additional men, with
whom she would have one son and one daughter each, so she
could become the mother of a whole new tribe.

Stocker and Kohler beat the girl once or twice daily. The
other men, called upon to help, at times were summoned by
telephone to participate in the torture and degradation of the
young girl.

The final scene followed a dinner on May 14, 1966, in
which the six cultists participated. Once again, Bernadette's
alleged "Devil's Pact" was discussed in detail, together with
her "desire to cause the death" of Stocker and Kohler. The
girl was sent to her room and ordered to crouch on her bed,
kneeling, resting on her elbows and hands, exposing her back-
side to the torturers.

According to the court testimony, as summarized in the
Swiss newspaper *Blick* (January 8, 1969), "an orgy of brutality began, in order to drive out the Devil—as the sadistic
cultist put it—and to make her feel the rightful anger of the
Lord." This account states that "the quietly whimpering girl
was beaten by all six 'devil exorcists' in succession, whereby
whips, canes and a plastic pipe were used to beat her on the
buttocks, back and extremities." More than 100 strokes fell
on her.

When, in her pain, the child lost control over her bowels,
she was forced to place excrement in her mouth and told to
"eat it." This resulted in a vomiting attack, and Kohler
pushed Bernadette into the bathtub. Finally, the young girl
had to wash her soiled clothing in the water near the house
and was permitted to go to bed. She died the next morning;
according to the Judicial-Medical Institute at Basel, her death
was due to an embolism of the lungs. Her body showed numerous bruises, abrasions, and broken skin. She died a virgin.

The hold which Stocker-Kohler had over the Hasler family
is further dramatized by the fact that Bernadette's parents

agreed to a scheme whereby Bernadette's body would be taken to the Barmettler home, in the village of Wangen, in order to avoid police attention.

The Haslers originally became enmeshed in the sexually sadistic delusions of Stocker and Kohler after they met in 1956. The Haslers believed the latter's messianic claims, which led to the establishment of an "International Family Society for the Advancement of Peace," supposedly designed to prepare for an "end of the world." The Hasler home was known as "Noah's Ark" among the schoolmates of the Hasler girls.

Bernadette's father, Josef Hasler, said at the trial, "I could not know, then, that this was the beginning of a road of suffering for our daughter." Hasler maintained that Stocker and Kohler estranged them from their daughter and persuaded them to turn over their second daughter, Madeleine, as well. The girls were not permitted to speak to their parents, but restricted to the "godly" education offered by their "Holy Parents." After Bernadette's death, the father went to rescue Madeleine from Stocker-Kohler. He said that he had literally to "tear her away from there," and that "she no longer regarded us as her parents; she had only eyes and ears for her 'Holy Parents,' Stocker and Kohler. After we told her of the torture death of Bernadette, her eyes opened. She told us that even the smallest children in that home were beaten to a pulp."

The shockingly successful brainwashing techniques applied by the "Holy Family" enslaved the Haslers as well as others. The team censored all mail. They took control of all monetary transactions and doled out food to the family. They used their Mercedes 300 for "missionary trips." Hasler recalled: "Hour-long prayers became brainwashing sessions. Until the early morning hours, satanic words were poured out and then we were ordered to be silent. I could no longer speak to my wife, as I would otherwise lose God's forgiveness. When my wife had to go to the hospital, because of a premature birth, I was forbidden to visit her."

Bernadette's father, slowly emerging from the grip of the "Holy Family" that caused the tragic death of his daughter, noted that he had "lost practically everything" and that "only debts remained." Asked about the trial, he said later, "If I had to judge those two today, I would beat them to a pulp and feed them to the pigs."

When the details of Bernadette's death were made known during the trial, her father cried out, "You have killed my child!" Paul Barmettler muttered, "Not killed, only beaten."

Mrs. Hasler, after lifting the nightgown from Bernadette's body and seeing the torture marks, had cried out and collapsed. But Magdalena Kohler blamed the Hasler parents: "You are guilty that Bernadette was possessed by the Devil. You did not bring her up right!" She tried to force Josef Hasler to take the guilt for his daughter's death upon himself: "If you refuse, you become a traitor to our Holy Work. Anyway, you will only have to serve one year, at worst."

Magdalena Kohler's fanaticism emerged in a statement she wrote one month before the trial, which took place in Zurich in January 1969. She said, "I have, in everything I did, acted under orders from God. All force, and all that has happened, was done on divine instructions. To avoid discipline, or faith, to withhold oneself from divine orders, leads the soul to punishment in hell and eternal damnation."

Speaking for the defense, Dr. Hans Meisser cited this statement to show that Magdalena was "a simpleminded woman, who grew up in an environment of narrow superstition and fear of eternal damnation. She is convinced that, one day, she will have to fight a duel with the Devil." He added that, while living secretly at the Hasler farm, the Kohler woman was "psychologically destroyed" and "believed more and more in her delusion, in her own supernatural powers and divine mission." The defense attorney added that the cultists had not meant to kill the young girl.

Another defense attorney, speaking of Emilio Bettio, said that his client was fully convinced that he was not beating Bernadette, but Lucifer. The lawyer pointed to the strong religious upbringing of the defendants and described Bettio as an "infantile, dependent" personality, that of one "who lived in constant fear of the eternal damnation that Stocker and Kohler preached with devastating effectiveness."

State Attorney John Lohner demanded penalties that would "serve as a warning to all those still enmeshed in superstitions and in abusing religious faith." He urged Catholic Church authorities to aid in "cleansing the soil that nurtures belief in and fear of the Devil, so that such crimes as that against Bernadette Hasler may never be repeated."

Speaking for the Roman Catholic Church, the Bishop of Chur, Dr. Johannes Vonderach, reaffirmed traditional concepts concerning the existence of the Devil, but said that the torturers and killers of Bernadette had violated Church principles in three ways: they had accepted totally imaginary "messages from beyond," had falsely accepted demonic "possession," and had acted against this mistaken condition on their own, with primitive and destructive means. Bishop Vonderach added: "Just as the Church separates itself from superstitious belief in miracles, it rejects a false belief in the Devil. However, as it regards the Devil seriously, on the basis of Holy Writ, it places itself doubly under the protection of the crucified Lord." The Bishop noted that the Church only very rarely, and when all scientific explanations have been exhausted, accepts the reality of demonic influence: in such cases, and only through a qualified priest, may a prayer of exorcism be uttered, whose wording has been fixed by the *Rituale Romanum*; "the bodily use of force is excluded."

Public opinion in Switzerland, and particularly in Zurich, was aroused by the "witch trial in reverse." Letters and telephone calls urged severe punishment of the accused, and extreme threats were directed against Magdalena Kohler. Threats stating that the court house would be blown up, unless "the most severe punishment were fixed," were made in anonymous telephone calls. On February 4, 1969, the court sentenced Josef Stocker and Magdalena Kohler to 10 years in prison, while Bettio was sentenced to four years and the Barmettler brothers to three-and-a-half.

The trial did not explore the background of this unique twentieth-century witchcraft trial in detail, because prosecution and defense were largely concerned with the intent and actual crime of the defendants. However, in terms of religious pathology and the impact of psychological delusion on criminal behavior, a look at the development of the Stocker-Kohler cult reveals some interesting successive steps: early and increasing fanaticism, messianic delusions, the creation of a self-centered cult that set its members apart from reality, and the acting-out of sexual sadism.

The initial role of the Carmelite nun Stella, known as "Little Star," remains oddly obscure; this is partly due to the fact that she was removed early on to a cloistered existence in Augsburg, Germany. Her original name had been Olga Endres; she met Stocker and Kohler while the two were visiting Jerusalem in 1956 during a "pilgrimage." Stella had, for a number of years, claimed that she was receiving messages of instruction directly from Jesus Christ. It had become her practice to transcribe these "Messages from the Savior" to typewritten form. Her superiors either failed to recognize her apparent mediumist psychosis or regarded these messages, in some manner, as genuine or at least uplifting.

Stocker and Kohler were only too willing to accept her "revelations." Josef Stocker had joined the Palottine Order in 1929. (By the time of trial, he was severely ill with diabetes: his left leg had to be amputated below the knee, as had the toes of his right foot.) The joint "pilgrimage" of Stocker and Kohler included a visit to the Shrine of Fatima in Portugal, where they claimed that a vision had prompted them to visit the Near East. In Jerusalem, Stella belonged to the Congregation of Borromaes. Her mediumistic or pseudomediumistic messages were regarded by her superiors, at least temporarily, as "an extraordinary mystical phenomenon," rather than as an expression of psychopathology. (At the time of the trial, Stella said she regarded this period of her activities as "total nonsense" and doubted the validity of the "Messages from the Savior." However, one church historian, Professor Dr. Walter Nigg, described her role as being, "if not in a judicial sense, at least in a religious sense that of a key person, who bears a heavy moral guilt that cannot simply be eradicated by calculated disregard of the past.")

Stella, Stocker, and Kohler returned together from the Near East to Europe. Their development into a pseudofamily, with Stella as the "child" of Josef and Magdalena had odd psychological overtones; Stella was even ordered by Magdalena to play with dolls. Magdalena Kohler testified that "Herr Stocker was the Father, I was the Mother, and Stella the Child." She added that "God" had ordered her to buy Stella a red teddy bear.

This *ménage à trois* continued to exist in Singen, Germany, where the newly formed apocalyptic cult prepared for the end of the world. One room remained empty, reserved for the Pope. Magdalena said: "It was supposed to be his place of refuge, once the final catastrophe crashed down on mankind."

The Palottine Order instructed Stocker to cease these activities, but he refused and was excommunicated. Stella was ordered to return to a nunnery. Stocker twice succeeded in taking her away from the cloister, and she was twice returned to it. By then, Stella had been reduced to infantilism. Magdalena Kohler had taken the reins for the "Holy Family's" ride to disaster. Stella recalled that the cult headquarters agreed with her less than the cloistered existence: "Times were not as good as here in the Cloister. I no longer had a will of my own, and I was in constant inner fear. I was spoken to as if I were a child." She added: "Today I no longer play with dolls. I no longer write Messages from the Savior. I was suffering from a malignant delusion."

But, back in 1957 and 1958, Stella prophesied the end of the world, complete with a rain of brimstone. According to Professor Nigg, the road from the cult's "Holy Work" of saving souls to the death of Bernadette was "not a straight path, which by some intrinsic force had to lead to this immensely tragic end." The church historian, formerly at the University of Zurich, defines the fate of Bernadette as follows:

"Like a witch in the Middle Ages, Bernadette began to play the game that had been forced upon her, so that, defiantly, she accused herself of the most repulsive sexual misdeeds with the Devil . . . Abandoned by all human sentiment, without the slightest support, she died alone in the night, without any hope of divine aid, an expectation that had long before been destroyed within her very soul."

12. Lurancy Vennum's Twin Spirit

Susy Smith

No volume concerned with inexplicable psychic experiences involving children would be complete without an account of the spirit control exercised by Mary Roff, who had died at the age of nineteen, over the body and psyche of a neighbor's child, Lurancy Vennum. Susy Smith is the author of some thirty books, including Confessions of a Psychic, Life is Forever, *and* The Power of the Mind. *She lives in Tucson, Arizona, but travels widely on lectures and research projects.*

The case of Lurancy Vennum shows that a hysterical child who is demon possessed can be rehabilitated if a wise spirit is allowed to take her in hand. It is probably the best incident in history to indicate that it is sometimes possible to gain control of the evil spirits who influence a susceptible child without resorting to exorcism or other drastic measures.

We are indebted to the careful observation and assistance of Dr. E. W. Stevens of Janesville, Wisconsin, for a careful investigation and reportage of this case while it was still occurring. Dr. Stevens published his account in a pamphlet entitled "The Watseka Wonder" and it was later reprinted in the *Religio-Philosophical Journal*, December 20, 1890. The journal's editor accompanied it with the statement: "We took great pains before and during publication to obtain full corroboration of the astounding facts from unimpeachable and competent witnesses."

The story, as it was thus recorded, indicates that for the last six months of the year 1877 a thirteen-year-old girl named Mary Lurancy Vennum of Watseka, Illinois, had recurrent "fits." They started out innocuously enough. On July 11, 1877 the girl was unconscious for five hours. Next day, the trance recurred, but she was able to describe her sensations to her family even though lying as if dead. She said she could see heaven and the angels, and a little brother and sister and others who had died. These trances, occasionally passing into ecstasy, when she claimed to be in heaven, occurred several times a day up to the end of January 1878. Then the "demons" took over, as they often do in such cases; the poor child was possessed, frequently by a very low type of spirit who made her act violently and do hateful things. Friends of her family insisted that she was insane, and urged that she be put away.

There had been a girl named Mary Roff who also lived in Watseka and had become similarly possessed. She had died at the age of almost nineteen, when Lurancy was only fifteen months old. Mary had suffered from fits frequently from the age of six months. These gradually increased in violence. She also had periods of despondency. During one such period she cut her arm with a knife until she fainted. Five days of raving mania followed. Afterward, she recognized no one, and seemed to lose all her natural senses; but when blindfolded she could read and do everything as if able to see. A few days later she returned to her normal condition. Soon, however, the fits became worse, and she died during one of them in July 1865.

Because Mary's case was so similar to Lurancy's, her parents, Mr. and Mrs. Asa B. Roff, visited the Vennums and offered their assistance. It was they who recommended asking Dr. Stevens, a prominent spiritualist of the area, for help.

This gentleman, a complete stranger to the family, was introduced by Mr. Roff at four o'clock one afternoon in February, no other persons being present but the Vennums. The girl sat near the stove, in a straight chair, her elbows on her knees, her hands under her chin, feet curled up on the chair, eyes staring, looking in every way like an old hag. She sat for a time in silence, until Dr. Stevens moved his chair. Then, she savagely warned him not to come nearer. She appeared sullen and crabbed, calling her father "Old Black Dick" and her mother "Old Granny." She refused to be touched, even to shake hands, and was reticent and sullen with all except the doctor, with whom she entered freely into conversation. When asked why she acted like that, she replied that he was a spiritual doctor and would understand her.

She described herself first as an old woman named Katrina

Hogan. Then, apparently, she was possessed by the spirit of a young man who said his name was Willie Canning. After some disjointed talk, she had another fit, which Dr. Stevens relieved by hypnotizing her. Lurancy grew calm, then, and said that she had been controlled by evil spirits. Dr. Stevens suggested she should try to have a better spirit "control," to protect her from other spirits, and encouraged her to find one. She then mentioned the names of several deceased persons, and said that there was one who particularly wanted to help her, named Mary Roff.

Mr. Roff, who was still present, assured Lurancy that Mary was good and intelligent, and that she could be depended upon. He told Lurancy of Mary's experiences that had been similar to hers. The child, after due deliberation and counsel with the spirits she said were there assembled, stated that Mary would possess her in order to protect her from the former wild and unreasonable influences.

The very next day, the spirit of Mary Roff moved into the body of Lurancy Vennum, and remained there almost continuously for nearly four months. Once Mary entered Lurancy's body, she felt strange in the Vennum home, where she knew no one, and asked to be allowed to return to her parents' home. Mr. Vennum called at Mr. Roff's office and said, "She seems like a child real homesick, wanting to go see her Pa and Ma and her brothers."

And so the girl was taken to the house of the Roffs, where she felt more at home. For the next three months this child, who looked like thirteen-year-old Lurancy Vennum, spoke, acted, thought, and remembered like the eighteen-year-old Mary Roff who had died twelve years before—happy and contented in her borrowed body. She seemed to know everything and every person Mary had known in the past. She recognized and called by name those who were friends of her family. She remembered scores, yes, hundreds of incidents that had transpired during Mary's life.

A few instances, from the numerous examples Dr. Stevens has reported, illustrate this phenomenon. One evening, while the child was out in the yard, Mr. Roff suggested that his wife find a certain velvet headdress Mary had worn during the last year before she died. He told her to lay it out, say nothing about it, and see whether it would be recognized. Mrs. Roff readily found it and placed it on a stand. When Lurancy-Mary came in, she exclaimed as she approached the stand, "Oh, there is my headdress I wore when my hair was short!" She then asked, "Ma, where is my box of letters? Have you got them yet?" Mrs. Roff dug out a box stored in the attic. Examining it, the girl said, "Oh, Ma, here is a collar I tatted. Why didn't you show me my letters and things before?"

One day a Mrs. Parker, who had been a neighbor of the Roffs when they had lived in Middleport in 1852, and next door to them in Watseka in 1860, came in with her daughter-in-law, Nellie Parker. Mary immediately recognized both ladies, "Auntie Parker" and "Nellie," as in former days. In conversation with Mrs. Parker, Mary asked, "Do you remember how Nervie and I used to come to your house and sing?" No one had mentioned this until Mary did, but she and her sister Minerva used to go to the Parker house and sit and sing with them.

In conversation with Dr. Stevens about her former life, the girl spoke of cutting her arm and asked him if he had ever seen where she did it. On receiving a negative answer, she slipped up her sleeve as if to exhibit the scar, but suddenly arrested the movement; she said quickly, "Oh, this is not the arm; that one is in the ground." Then she told him where it was buried, and how she had attended her own funeral. But she had not felt bad about it, she said, being glad to get out of a body over which she so seldom had control.

Some of the best accounts of incidents during this period of occupation by a good spirit of the formerly possessed Mary Lurancy Vennum have been given by Dr. Richard Hodgson, who, as Research Director of the Society for Psychical Research at that time, discovered Dr. Stevens' paper and decided to investigate the "Watseka Wonder" while people who remembered were still alive. When Dr. Hodgson visited Mrs. Minerva Alter, Mary's sister, she told him many curious stories. She assured him that the mannerisms and behavior of the child during the three months she was under the control of Mary Roff had quite strikingly resembled Mary's. The real Lurancy had barely met Mrs. Alter, but as Mary she embraced her affectionately and called her "Nervie." This was Mary's pet name for her sister, by which Mrs. Alter had not been called since Mary's death.

While Lurancy-Mary stayed at Mrs. Alter's home, almost every hour of the day some trifling incident of Mary's life was recalled by her. One morning she said, "Right over there by the currant bushes is where Allie greased the chicken's eye." This incident had happened several years before Mary's death. Mrs. Alter remembered very well their cousin Allie treating the sick chicken's eye with oil. Allie now lived in Peoria, Illinois; Lurancy had never known her.

One morning, Mrs. Alter asked the girl if she remembered an old dog they had owned. Lurancy replied, "Yes, he died over there," pointing to the exact spot where the pet had breathed his last. Such things are not inordinately elegant as conversation goes, but as evidence of identity and personal memory, they are highly significant. The Roff family considered the many little things of this nature to be incontrovertible evidence that Mary was actually visiting them in this other body, no matter how strange the situation may have been.

During her stay with the Roff family, the child's physical condition continually improved, and she apparently built up resistance to the demonic forces which had previously controlled her. She was often invited and went with Mrs. Roff to visit the leading families of the city, who soon became satisfied that the girl was not crazy, but a fine well-mannered child.

It was on May 21, 1878 that Mary told her family Lurancy was now well enough to return to her own body. After a tearful farewell from the Roffs, Mary left, and Lurancy, once again, looked out of her own eyes! She was well from then on. The Roffs and Vennums had become friends—this experience of joint ownership of a daughter had, not surprisingly, brought them close together. For some years afterwards, until Lurancy married and left home, whenever the parents visited together Lurancy would go into a trance and allow Mary to control her body, so she could chat with her father and mother. Because Mary Roff's tenure had somehow strengthened her unconscious ability to resist the evil spirits, Lurancy was never again possessed against her will.

13. Never Again!

Martin Ebon

There is no clear dividing line between what parapsychologists classify as "poltergeist phenomena" and what, in some religio-cultural settings, might be regarded as "demon possession." The following report on one of the most widely publicized such cases in the recent past took place is a contemporary American home, and its inexplicable phenomena seemed to concentrate on, or originate with, a twelve-year-old boy. At one point, the father suggested that he might have "picked up" a destructive discarnate entity during a Caribbean voyage, but this was just one of many speculations concerning the basis for the disturbances in the house. The family members were agreed on one point, when looking back on the incidents that created nationwide publicity; asked whether they anticipated a return of the phenomena, they said, "Never again!"

On June 3, exactly five months after the first bottles "popped" at the home of James M. Herrmann in Seaford, Long Island, a reporter rang the doorbell of the attractive, quiet suburban house. It was difficult to imagine, under the shade trees of this small community in Nassau County, New York, that for more than a month this home had been the scene of an old-fashioned "poltergeist" haunting—with, to be sure, a good many modern touches in action and interpretation. This evening, the Herrmann family had returned from a vacation trip to the British West Indies: James Herrmann; his wife, Lucille; their fourteen-year-old daughter, Lucille; and their twelve-year-old son, James, Jr., whom everyone calls Jimmy. It was a well-deserved vacation. It followed five weeks of bottle-popping, furniture-hopping and bookcase-dropping, and three more months of hectic publicity, interviews, and investigations.

The time had come to assess, if possible, the effects of all these unsettling events on the Herrmann family. How did they now feel about those strange happenings that had mystified the nation, and that had been reported all over the globe?

Mr. and Mrs. Herrmann were sitting quietly in their living room, which had been the scene of a number of apparently inexplicable phenomena. They were undoubtedly grateful that the period of excitement and confusion had passed. Although it was early evening, both children were in bed.

But Mr. and Mrs. Herrmann were still in doubt as to the real cause of the phenomena that had made their household a center of nationwide attention. Frankly, they did not know what natural or supernatural "force" had balanced bottles on cartons, smashed a portable record player and thrown a 20-inch-high statue of the Virgin Mary across a bedroom.

The events had begun on February 3, 1958, and had stopped on March 10. On May 15, Dr. Karlis Osis, then Director of Research of the Parapsychology Foundation, following an investigation, reported in the Foundation's *Newsletter* that Jimmy "might have caused the disturbances by normal means if he so wished." Mr. and Mrs. Herrmann rejected this explanation; they were angry and hurt that anyone might suspect their boy of mischievous trickery. Had not Dr. J. G. Pratt, Associate Director, Parapsychology Laboratory, Duke University, been quoted as saying that the incidents were "not a hoax perpetrated by a member of the family"? And Dr. J. L. Woodruff, Department of Psychology, College of the City of New York, had left the matter open in the Journal of the American Society for Psychical Research, stating that the question of "normal involvement of the children" was "largely a matter of opinion."

It was quiet in the house on 1648 Redwood Path. The inquiring reporters were gone. The television cameras had been trucked away. Letters were still coming in; the Herrmanns were trying to be conscientious in answering serious inquiries and suggestions. As Mr. Herrmann put it, "We are beginning to repair the damage that was done, and we hope we won't have to go through all that again . . ."

What were the events that had done this damage to the

Herrmann household? They began on February 3, at 3 P.M. During the next two hours, six screw-top bottles opened, fell over and spilled their contents. The bottles were located in four different rooms. One contained holy water, another nail polish remover, another rubbing alcohol and the others liquified starch and bleach.

Mrs. Herrmann telephoned her husband in his office at Air France, the airline for which he works as an inter-line liaison executive. She told him that "all the bottles in the house are blowing their tops." As Mr. Herrmann recalls it, in Jimmy's room "a porcelain Davy Crockett, a wooden gondola and a plastic angel all fell to the floor and broke. The crucifix fell off our wall and a bottle of holy water turned over and spilled." (The Herrmanns are a Roman Catholic family.)

On February 6, bottles opened once again, spilled their contents and, above all, divested themselves of their screw-on tops. Also, a bottle of bleach was said to have "jumped" out of a cardboard box for the second time. The plastic angel, once again, fell from its position on a shelf. The next day, about half a dozen bottles opened up.

While the family was sitting at the Sunday breakfast table, February 9, the events were all but forgotten. In Mr. Herrmann's words, "Then, bang! The perfume goes. The holy water goes. While we're cleaning up, we hear everything letting go in the bathroom. . . ." Mr. Herrmann notified the Seventh Precinct of the local police, and police officer James Hughes came to the house.

The phenomena continued on the 11th: a small perfume bottle lost its atomizer cap and fell on its side; this took place in the room occupied by Lucille, the daughter. In the basement, a turpentine can that had fallen over twice on February 9 toppled to its side. The police assigned Detectives Joseph Tozzi and Sgt. Bert McConnell to the case. Mr. Tozzi removed the perfume bottle for analysis by the Police Laboratory at Mineola, L. I.

Next day, at the suggestion of the police detectives, supervised by Assistant Chief Inspector Francis Looney, the family refilled several bottles with water. They obtained twelve-ounce and six-ounce bottles and placed them, filled, in spots within the house that had previously been scenes of bottle-popping or other incidents.

On February 13, an eight-ounce bottle of holy water appeared to "throw" its screwed-on cap upward. This bottle had been freshly filled, following a previous "explosion." Inspector Frank Pribyl, chief of the Police Laboratory at Mineola, L. I., reported that no "foreign agents" had been found in the bottle examined earlier. The Long Island Lighting Company installed a high-frequency vibration detecting apparatus in the Herrmann home. The device was described by company engineers as "so sensitive that it could record the rappings of human knuckles on the floor at the other end of the cellar." No vibrations were recorded, while the vibration detector remained installed overnight. "Decoy" bottles, filled with water, remained undisturbed throughout the next day.

On February 15, James Herrmann reported that a bottle of holy water, knocked over once before, was found lying on its side in the master bedroom. He said: "I had just gone into the room with my son and daughter and we noticed that this bottle had fallen. I rushed over to the perfume bottle to see if anything had happened to that. It was hot, as if lukewarm water was in it." In the evening, a visiting cousin, Miss Marie Murtha, and the two children reported that they had seen a porcelain figure of a colonial woman move through the air.

A plastic angel moved from Jimmy's night table on February 16 and was reported to have "flown" about four feet through the air and struck a statuette of Davy Crockett. A bottle had fallen. I rushed over to the perfume bottle to see if as well as a lamp in Jimmy's room and another one in the master bedroom were seemingly knocked to the floor.

After five days of quiescence, a bleach bottle "exploded" its screw cap on February 20, and Detective Tozzi was called to the house. At 8:30 a crash was heard and the porcelain figurine of a colonial man was reported to have flown from an end table and to have crashed against a nearby secretary table. The impact caused a noticeable dent in the wood. Shortly after 9 P.M. a bowl, filled with sugar, was reported to have left a dinette table, hitting a door and breaking into pieces. Detective Tozzi observed part of the bowl's movement, from the hall. Later on, in the basement, Detective Tozzi observed a horse-and-rider bronze figure move from the staircase and land at his feet.

On February 21, the Herrmann family, following the events of the previous day, decided to leave its residence, at least temporarily. They moved to the nearby home of relatives. Meanwhile, police cooperated with the Herrmann family in placing a revolving cap over the chimney of its house, designed to prevent air currents that might displace household items.

The Herrmann family returned home February 23. In the living room, a figurine fell; in the master bedroom a lamp tumbled down; in Jimmy's room a heavy chest of drawers fell over.

On February 24, following a rumbling noise, a heavy chest of drawers was discovered tipping over in Jimmy's room shortly before 5 P.M. Later on, an ashtray on a cocktail table moved toward a secretarial desk; at 8:30 P.M. a globe was seen moving through the air. At 9 P.M. a heavy book case was said to have moved at a 45-degree angle and to have "dumped all its books."

Shortly after midnight a picture drawn by Jimmy fell off the wall in his room. In the same room a figure fell down and knocked over a picture taken at Mr. and Mrs. Herrmann's wedding. A statue was reported to have "smashed" into the frame of a mirror. About 6 P.M. of February 25, a portable phonograph "crashed" into the woodwork of the basement staircase. Later, a metal bread plate moved off the dining room table.

Next day, a mobile receiver-transmitter was brought to the house from the Rocky Point station of the Radio Corporation of America. The device was described as capable of receiving radio signals from 15 kilocycles to 220 megacycles. RCA technicians Lester E. Rider and Lowell E. Fletcher, who brought the receiver, stated they would examine the various wavebands for "unusual or phenomenal signals which may be passing through the area." At the same time the Building Commissioner of Hempstead, L. I., Fred J. Klaess, together with building examiners, checked the house for possible structural irregularities that might have contributed to the phenomena reported. Both investigations failed to uncover any unusual conditions.

On March 2, a lamp in the parents' bedroom fell to the floor, and the centerpiece on the dining room table crashed against the cabinet. At 8:00 P.M. a picture in the room of James, Jr. fell to the floor. At 8:45 P.M. the globe flew from the same room. At 10:10 P.M. the night table beside Jimmy's bed fell over on its side, together with a lamp that was on it. Mr. Herrmann observed part of its fall, with a flashlight.

Two days later, John Gold, New York correspondent of

the London *Evening News,* reported that about 5 P.M. he saw a flashbulb move from an end table in the living room and strike a wall about twelve feet away. Following this, three or four knocks were heard coming from the kitchen wall. Shortly afterwards, a noise was heard in the basement. A bleach bottle was found "balanced" on top of a cardboard soap carton, with its cap on the floor, about two feet away. Then, a glass centerpiece was reported to have moved from the dining room table to a cupboard, breaking a piece of molding. At 6 P.M. a heavy bookcase toppled over in the basement where Jimmy was doing his homework.

On March 5, a world globe, which had figured in two previous incidents, appeared to have moved from the room of James, Jr. and landed in the hall. The event took place in the evening, after Jimmy had gone to bed. Next day, while Mrs. Herrmann was preparing breakfast, a coffee table overturned in the living room.

Intermittent incidents continued to occur up to March 10. No fully satisfactory hypothesis was developed nor did the various physical and chemical investigations suggest direct cause. Scrutiny of the building structure indicated merely normal settling.

The events in the Herrmann home received wide-spread attention from newspapers, magazines, radio and television. Associated Press reports were carried by all major newspapers and items were carried in smaller newspapers and broadcast on radio stations throughout the country. Rather full accounts were carried by the New York *World-Telegram,* the *New York Times,* and the Long Island paper, *Newsday,* during the days when the events were most active.

Reports were carried in the following national magazines: *Newsweek,* on March 10 and 24; *Time,* on March 17, and a rather extensive article appeared in *Life,* March 17; it was reprinted in the *Reader's Digest's* June issue. An article appeared in the August issue of *Pageant.* Herrmann was interviewed on John Wingate's television show, "Night Beat," on March 18, and on the "Jack Parr Show," June 11.

He was also interviewed on the local New York radio program, "The Tex and Jinx Show" on WRCA, March 10. The whole family and the house were visited by Edward R. Murrow and the television cameras of CBS-TV, April 11, on the "Person to Person" program.

Several newspapers added editorial comments, mainly in a light and humorous vein.

Among major newspapers that commented editorially were the *Washington Post & Times Herald* and the *New York Times.* The Washington paper observed that "there aren't—so they say—many mysteries now left in the world, so we ought to be grateful for all those weird goings on turning the hitherto normal and peaceful household of Mr. and Mrs. James Herrmann of Seaford, Long Island, into a kind of 24-hour nightmare."

The *Times* quoted Hereward Carrington and Nandor Fodor as writing in their book *Haunted People* that "the poltergeist is not a ghost—it is a bundle of projected repressions." The paper, observing that the Seaford phenomena had apparently stopped, added:

"Whatever the case may be, the Herrmanns no longer have a poltergeist, much less any projected repressions. The poltergeist, or the projected repressions, will probably turn up somewhere else in due course of time. These things, whatever they are, get bored . . ."

The first full scholarly appraisal of the Seaford case was presented by Dr. Osis in the *Newsletter* of the Parapsychology Foundation under the title "An Evaluation of the Seaford 'Poltergeist' Case." The analysis was accompanied by a diagram of the Herrmanns' home, with tabulations showing the frequency and location of the incidents. Dr. Osis observed that "occurrences were most frequently associated with Jimmy's room, where they also first started. Next in frequency was the parental bedroom; then the dining room, where the children sometimes did their homework. Young Lucille's room and the play room in which she does part of her homework showed the least frequency."

Dr. Osis also noted that "the affected objects" seemed to have been "picked out from among others, without disturbing those adjacent to them." Thus, he concluded, "the disturbances in the house" did not appear "to have resulted from unguided action of physical variables," so that "we are definitely left with involvement of the human variables, normal or paranormal." Dr. Osis then proceeded to examine the possibility of normal or paranormal events.

As to the frequency of events, "Sundays definitely stand out over the rest of the week. Wednesdays and Fridays are very quiet. Whatever happened in Jimmy's room was, in 16 out of 18 cases, concentrated on Sundays and Mondays." On Saturday, when the family members were "kept busy" with household chores, "there were no disturbances," except for "a few in the evening when the work was over."

Dr. Osis also observed that the "peak frequency of phenomena" fell "just following the time of the children's return from school" and "disturbances during school hours occurred only on weekends." He concluded that "there is a close connection between Jimmy's activities, whereabouts and habits and the timing of the disturbances." He added: "We might further infer that Jimmy, in all probability, was the normal or paranormal cause of the events."

Dr. Osis then examined three hypotheses: that Jimmy might have unconsciously produced the phenomena by normal means; that he might have caused them consciously; or that the phenomena might have been produced by Jimmy's telekinetic influence on the disturbed objects. After examining ten of the most significant incidents, Dr. Osis concluded that "it is possible that every one of them could have been caused by normal means." He ended his report: "We have strong enough evidence that the boy might have caused the disturbances by normal means if he so wished. This gives us sufficient grounds upon which to reject the paranormal explanation."

This view contrasted sharply with that of Dr. J. G. Pratt of the Duke Parapsychology Laboratory as reported in the press. Dr. Pratt, pending a more detailed scholarly review, considered psychokinesis (defined by the Duke Laboratory as "the direct influence exerted on a physical system by a subject without any known intermediate physical energy or instrumentation") a possibility. Dr. Pratt applied a new concept, that of "Recurrent Spontaneous Psychokinesis" to the Seaford case. He was quoted by the Associated Press as saying: "There were numerous instances where the position of every member of the family was recorded when a bottle bounced or a cork flew off. I'm almost certain no hoax is involved." The United Press reported, following an interview with the Duke Laboratory's Assistant Director:

"Dr. Pratt said he had not been able yet to come up with an explanation for the mystery because there were 'too many angles' to consider. Exploring the possibility that mental power was responsible for the moving objects, he centered his attention on the Herrmann's son, 12 year old Jimmy. Psychokinesis, the ability to move objects with mental power, is believed more likely to appear in children, if it exists at all. Dr. Pratt said he was unable to say whether Jimmy had this strange power but he said he felt certain the boy was not playing a prank or lying."

Dr. Woodruff walked a scholarly tightrope in his report for the American Society for Psychical Research. He weighed the possibility of "intentional conscious human action of a non-parapsychological nature" against "manifestations of some kind of psi function," which would include psychokinesis. He felt that there is "small chance of arriving at a definite answer," adding that "it is perhaps most parsimonious for our discussion to attribute the incidents to Jimmy, whether normally or paranormally caused."

Dr. Woodruff noted, as had Dr. Osis, considerable domestic regimentation of the two Herrmann children; they received the rather small weekly allowance of 25 cents each, for which they had to account, and had to be in bed at an early hour nightly. Such discipline, considerably tighter than in an average household, could, in the eyes of the two authorities, result in underlying inter-personal tensions that might offer motivation for "normal" or "paranormal" incidents.

However, Dr. Woodruff concluded that "the events at Seaford, although providing an opportunity for almost 'on the spot' investigation, do not seem to provide the basis for a clear cut decision, regarding the presence or absence or parapsychological manifestations."

Several incidents that had achieved wide publicity appeared less striking when witnesses were questioned directly. Thus the New York *World Telegram & Sun* reported (February 26) that a portable phonograph was "hurtled twelve feet through the air and crashed against the cellar stairway." As this incident was repeated and re-told, the fact was generally omitted that, as reported in the same news dispatch, "Jimmy was sitting there all by his lonesome in one corner of the rumpus room, immersed in his homework," apparently sole witness of the event.

Mr. Herrmann, interviewed on the "Night Beat" television program (March 18) stated that, "One person actually saw [an object] start" in motion. This was Miss Marie Murtha whom he referred to as "a cousin of ours who was visiting the home." However, being interviewed by telephone, Miss Murtha stated that she did "not actually see the figurine fly up from the table." She and the two Herrmann children were watching television at the time; she had seen the figurine of a colonial woman start to wobble on an end table and then had seen something white, "like a feather," in the air above it. After the object had fallen to the floor, about five feet away, she stated that, "No one touched it," because Jimmy, who was the nearest person to the figure, would have had to lean over to reach it.

A third incident was reported in the *New York Times*, March 4, as follows: "John Gold, correspondent of the London *Evening News*, said he saw a flashbulb rise slowly from an eighteen-inch-high table in the living room at 5 P.M. It struck a wall about twelve feet away." In a later telephone interview, Mr. Gold said that he had not, in fact, seen the flashbulb rise from the table. He was standing at the door with Mrs. Herrmann, preparing to leave. The part of the living room from which the flight originated was not visible to him. He saw, as he put it, about "two-thirds" of the flight of the bulb, when it bounced off the living room wall. It was on this same occasion that a heavy bookcase fell over in the basement and Mr. Gold and Mrs. Herrmann discovered Jimmy standing in close proximity, and Gold noticed that Jimmy was "breathing hard," either, as he stated later, "out of fear or from doing a job of hard physical labor."

However, Mr. Herrmann feels that the radio-physical theory is the most likely, although he continues to be open-minded on theories of the cause of the events.

He told inquirers that, in his opinion, the objects in the house seem to have been driven in the same general direction within the house: diagonally, from north-west to south-east, and in a descending direction. In the numerous cases where their path did not follow this line directly, Mr. Herrmann theorizes that the objects might have been "bounced off" the unseen force, "like balls on a billiard table," where, by applying a spinning motion to a ball, and by hitting a second ball, this ball can be forced to move at an angle, up to 85 degrees.

Mr. Herrmann believes that such a force might have been caused by governmental experiments in such fields as radar and electronics, perhaps at the nearby U.S. Air Force Base on Mitchell Field.

As a result of the wide publicity which the Seaford case had in the press, on radio and television, the Herrmann family received a great number of letters that tried to explain the events. According to Mrs. Herrmann, the theories most frequently advanced fall into five major categories:

(1) A frequent suggestion, amusing to the family, is that "space men" may have been responsible for the mysterious happenings.

(2) Among religious explanations are those that interpret the happenings in terms of good and evil. Some correspondents suggest that the Devil must have been at work in Seaford; others feel that the family may have been guilty of some sin and are therefore being punished for it. A "good" force is sometimes suggested within the framework of Roman Catholic beliefs. It has been suggested, for instance, that Jimmy may be possessed of "miraculous powers," or that the force may emanate from a soul in Purgatory that desires prayer to reach Heaven.

(3) The traditional "poltergeist" idea of a spirit entity was advanced in various forms. Some correspondents felt that a malevolent spirit may be causing the incidents, while others think that the restless spirit of a person "buried under the house" may be responsible.

(4) The parapsychological thesis that psychokinesis is involved was mentioned in a number of letters.

(5) The theory of electro-magnetic forces, which Mr. Herrmann favors, was mentioned frequently.

Mrs. Herrmann spent some time reading literature that may throw light on the series of incidents. She considered the possibility that Jimmy may have been able to move objects, without knowing it, by "mind powers." However, this explanation does not convince her. As her husband put it: "Jimmy would have to devote his life to developing mental powers, like an Indian fakir, in order to move even a cigarette box a couple of inches."

While Mr. Herrmann stuck to electro-magnetism as a likely explanation, Mrs. Herrmann did not completely exclude the possibility of spirit agency. Considering the fact that, historically, a restless spirit is frequently considered the origin of such incidents, very little consideration seems to have been given to this age-old hypothesis, in this case.

Half-jokingly, Mr. Herrmann recalled that, not long before the incidents began, he had returned from a journey to the

Caribbean. Had "something" attached himself to him—Haitian loa or a Jamaican spirit entity? After briefly considering this possibility, he noted that a less esoteric explanation would be much more satisfactory. Meanwhile, Mrs. Herrmann looked around her well-ordered living room, with nothing more other-worldly in sight than a television screen, with the hope, "We're keeping our fingers crossed that it won't start all over again!"

14. The Illfurth Boys

Hans Petersen

Few cases of diabolical possession are recorded in detail, but that of the Illfurth Boys is an exception. Over a period of four years, two young brothers were apparently possessed by the Devil, and ecclesiastical efforts to exorcise them were at first fruitless. Only after lengthy and frustrating exorcism rites, which disrupted not only the boys' immediate family, but the whole parish, were the youngsters freed. Mr. Petersen has studied original parish records and relevant analyses in order to provide the following summary.

"While lying in their bed, the children used to turn to the wall, paint horrible Devil faces on it, and then speak to the faces and play with them. If, while one of the possessed was asleep, a rosary was placed on his bed, he would immediately hide under the covers and refuse to come out of hiding until the rosary was removed. At times, when a boy sat on a chair, both chair and boy were lifted off the ground and, without damage to either, would be thrown across the room; the chair might wind up in one corner and the child in another. At times, their bodies became bloated as if about to burst; when this happened, the boy would vomit, whereby yellow foam, feathers, and seaweed would come out of his mouth. Often, their clothes were covered with evil smelling feathers."

This description appears in the records of the Roman Catholic parish of the town of Illfurth, some eight miles from the city of Mulhouse, Alsace. The two boys who passed through four years of diabolical possession were Theobald and Joseph Bruner, sons of a farmer. Their possession began in September 1865, when Joseph was almost eight years old (he was born on April 29, 1857) and Theobald not quite ten (he was born on August 21, 1855). The pastoral archives give these details from the early period of their possession:

"During the first two years, while largely confined to bed, the two boys entangled their legs every two or three hours in an unnatural way. They knotted them so intricately that it was impossible to pull them apart. And yet, suddenly, they could untangle them with lightning speed. At times the boys stood simultaneously on their heads and legs, bent backwards, their bodies arched high. No amount of outside pressure could bring their bodies into a normal position—until the Devil saw fit to give these objects of his torture some temporary peace."

It is apparent from this description that the parish priest, Father Karl Brey, was convinced that the children were actually possessed by the Devil. His account provides details that strongly suggest forces being at work with the Bruner boys which exceeded anything which could simply be attributed to pranks, a high-spirited hoax, or mere boyish trickery. Assuming the correctness of the description, some of the boys' actions and contortions would seem to be outside their physical capabilities. Also, their tendency to identify themselves with diabolical forces, such as painting Devil faces on the wall and talking to their drawings, indicate attitudes in direct contrast to that of the firmly religious Bruner household. The parish record notes that, when they were outdoors, Joseph and Theobald "were able to climb trees with the agility of cats" and managed to "reach the thinnest branches without falling to the ground."

A unique heat phenomenon was noted during the possession period. "At times," the record states, "the room in which the children lived was filled with intolerable heat." Although there was no separate stove in the boys' room, it became so hot that no one was able to stay in it. Father Brey commented that "their mother, who shared the room with them," unable to stand the heat, used to get up and sprinkle holy water on the bed, after which "the temperature lowered and she was able to rest."

In retrospect, the fact that the mother shared the room with the boys and was a strict, pious woman, suggests psychological family stresses which today might have prompted a priest to recommend different living arrangements. It is obvious, too, that such actions as placing a rosary on the boys' bed amounted to religio-psychological provocation—directed either at the boys or the Devil himself.

The diabolical nature of the possession and the very firm religious attitude of the Bruner family can be gauged by the fact that, according to the record, the boys hid under a table or bed or jumped out the window when "a priest or a pious Catholic" came to visit. On the other hand, when someone arrived who was "not a devout Christian," the boys showed great pleasure and shouted, "Here is one of ours; if only everyone were like that!" It can be assumed that such incidents tended to draw a sharp line of demarkation between the Bruner family and other members of the parish or the Illfurth community. No doubt, Mrs. Bruner and Father Brey shared attitudes in direct contrast to those expressed by the possessed boys.

The possession phenomena were so disruptive that the priest and parents agreed on a formal exorcism of Joseph and Theobald as the only possible solution for their condition. They decided that the St. Charles Orphanage at Schiltigheim, near Strasbourg, would be the appropriate facility. St. Charles, operated by nuns, had as its superior one Father Stumpf, who functioned as exorcist in the Bruner case.

Theobald, the older of the boys, was first sent to St. Charles. "The Devil within him remained silent for three days," the parish record states, but appeared on the fourth day around 8 P.M., saying "I have come and I am in a rage."

One of the attending nuns, asked, "And who are you?"

"I am the Lord of Darkness," was the answer.

We are told that the voice resembled that of "a calf being choked." The record continues:

"When he was angry, the boy could look fear-inspiring. At such times, Theobald recognized no one, not even his mother. He tore his clothing and destroyed everything he could lay his hands on, until he was at last subdued. If he was given a piece of clothing into which a religious medal had been sewn, he immediately tore away the lining and pushed the blessed object out. He also became deaf at times and even laughed at Herr Stumpf [the exorcist] who had fired a pistol right next to the boy's ears. He said, 'He is trying to shoot and can't even manage that.' "

One of the criteria used to separate genuine diabolical possession from other disturbances is supernatural knowledge. Over and over, possessed people are credited with knowing facts outside the range of human sensory perception. Once, the two Bruner boys were visited by a priest and by the mayor of Illfurth, but only the mayor came up to their room. They had not seen the priest arrive, but yelled immediately, "The fellow in the black coat has come. We won't say a thing!" They then jumped around crazily and danced defiantly, stamping their feet on the floor.

The Illfurth parish record also states that "Theobald several times predicted the death of a person correctly," and adds: "Two hours before the death of a Frau Müller, the boy knelt on his bed and acted as if he were ringing a mourning bell. Another time he did the same thing for a whole hour. When he was asked for whom he was ringing, the boy answered, 'For Gregor Kunegel.' As it happened, Kunegel's daughter was visiting in the house. Shocked and angry, she told Theobald, 'You liar, my father is not even ill. He is working on the new boys' seminary building as a mason.' Theobald answered, 'That may be, but he just had a fall. Go ahead and check on it!' The facts bore him out. The man had fallen from a scaffold, breaking his neck. This happened at the very moment that Theobald made the bell-ringing motions. No one in Illfurth had been aware of the accident."

With recent advances in the study of telepathy, some contemporary Roman Catholic theologians might now attribute both instances of apparent supernatural knowledge to thought transmission. One Vatican authority on possession, exorcism, and parapsychology, Monsignor Corrado Balducci, has expressed the view that such extrasensory qualities as telepathy and clairvoyance should be treated as "natural" human abilities when seeking to establish possession. Balducci feels that only when all normal channels of knowledge can be excluded, including such forms of ESP as telepathy, should possession be regarded as truly genuine. Theobald's apparent knowledge of Kunegel's fatal accident might today be categorized as "crisis telepathy," presumably from the dying person to the telepathic recipient; crisis telepathy cases are the most numerous recorded in the mind-to-mind communication category.

More complex, either as telepathy or clairvoyance, is another Illfurth incident. The mayor of a small town near Strasbourg one Sunday decided to visit the Bruner boys. With him were several members of the municipal council. The group was concerned that the Devil might be able to communicate the background of their visit to Theobald and Joseph Bruner; as one of them put it, "It is said that the Devil is able to tell one the truth." The mayor suggested that the men first go to confession, take communion, and visit Illfurth only afterwards, so "the Devil can't hold anything against us."

Having taken these precautions, the group came to the Bruner house, entered the boys' room, and either Theobald or Joseph said: "Look at that! There's the mayor of X and others from the municipal council. Well, you didn't trust the weather, and so you went to church yesterday and had them scrape the dirt from your conscience. Right? But one of you didn't do it properly. He stole the turnips." The council member to whom this accusing remark was addressed, apparently involving fraud concerning a vegetable shipment, shouted, "Yes, but I put down the money for it." The boy answered "But these people never did get the money, after all." Following this, the parish record observes, the gentleman beat a hasty retreat.

Possession is frequently accompanied by phenomena that can range from mysterious knocking and scraping sounds (similar to those associated with so-called poltergeist phenomena) to unpleasant smells or the presence of pests and parasites. Several families who had been particularly attentive to Theobald and Joseph, experienced such upsetting sounds and movements. Their houses and stables had to be blessed several times before the phenomena disappeared.

One neighbor visited the boys after he had experienced a great deal of noise in the upper rooms of his house. He was welcomed by the boys, speaking with the Devil's voice, saying, "Did you hear us last night? Well, we've certainly managed to carry on plenty!" While he was being exorcised at the Schiltigheim orphanage, Theobald told a guardian nun, "I have lice." She looked the boy over and found "innumerable red lice on the head of the possessed." This, of itself, would not have been significant, but the parasitical insects kept on multiplying mysteriously: "Together with three other people, she began to treat the child's head with comb and brush. But the more vermin they eliminated, the more appeared. The priest finally went to get some holy water and poured it over the boy's head, saying 'In the name of the Holy Trinity, I order you to leave this child!' From that moment on, the lice disappeared. The same method helped against a similar infestation that had begun to infect Joseph."

Other side effects of the Illfurth possession case were more serious for the boys and their family. The record contains the following passage:

"Theobald was being persecuted by a hateful-looking animal: it had the beak of a duck, its hands were like claws, and its body was covered by dirty feathers. As soon as the boy saw the monster floating over his bed, he cried out in terror. The entity threatened to choke him to death. In desperation, the boy threw himself on it and pulled out its feathers. This occurred some twenty to thirty times, always in broad daylight and in the presence of several people from all levels of society. The feathers had a repulsive smell, and when burned left no ash."

This account suggests that only Theobald saw the animal that was "persecuting" him, but that the feathers he "pulled out" were physically tangible objects that were seen and handled by others. The appearance of odd and sometimes dangerous objects, such as needles or nails, is frequently a feature in possession cases. The Illfurth case also had these elements:

"On other occasions, the boys experienced a painful sort of piercing and itching all over their bodies. From their clothing they pulled an enormous amount of feathers and seaweed that eventually covered the whole floor. No matter how often their shirts and outer clothing were changed, new feathers and seaweed would appear. These feathers, which covered their bodies in some inexplicable way, filled the air with such a stench that they had to be burned without delay."

Among the factors that count against the hypotheses that the Illfurth boys were merely engaged in some elaborate hoax are the elements of self-deprivation which this would have encompassed. In alleged possession cases reported from Brazil and Haiti in the recent past are many instances where the supposedly possessed person asks to be given food, liquor, or cigars—all in the name of the possessing entity. Theobald and Joseph, on the other hand, passed up food of which they were quite fond, saying "The Devil won't let me eat it!" At times, in line with other possession cases, they ate very little. Conversely, one of them might eat a whole basket of apples in one sitting. On the whole, their diet was fairly normal, however.

The boys' physiology was, of course, affected by all these phenomena. At times, Theobald's body was so bloated that—

as the parish record notes—strong men were incapable of flattening his belly, but when the priest sprinkled holy water on him, the boy's body took on its normal proportions.

Those who have seen the motion picture *The Exorcist* are familiar with the taunting arrogance attributed to the Devil in possession cases. His worst taunts and filthiest language are, of course, directed against the exorcist who seeks to oust the Devil from the body of the possessed person. In the case of Theobald, he returned from an exorcism at a church one evening, and as he lay on his bed the Devil spoke through him and said, "I am furious." When he was asked where Theobald had been taken, earlier in the day, the answer was, "To a pigsty." When he was asked, "Who took you there?" he replied, "That thickheaded vagabond." This description apparently referred to the orphanage's gardener, who had escorted the boy to the exorcism ritual.

That same evening, the Devil-in-the-boy was asked by a nun, "Who else was there?" and answered, "You." The possessing entity then cursed and grumbled. Asked next, "Who sprinkled holy water on you?" he answered, "The bitch who looks after the little pups." This was regarded as a reference to the nun in charge of Theobald and Joseph, who had followed his brother to the orphanage. When asked why he hadn't let Theobald eat his dinner that evening, the Devil replied, "The little runt didn't need anything. I got all I wanted in the pigsty."

The dialogue continued, with the Devil's language becoming more and more vile, more and more blasphemous. Looking back, this question-and-answer interlude strikes one as a violation of the traditional exorcism code, the *Rituale Romanum*, which specifically asks exorcists to avoid getting into a discussion or argument with whatever diabolic, demonic, or evil-spirit entity might possess an individual. The impression cannot be avoided that the nun questioning the Devil was overstepping the line of appropriate conduct, and may even have enjoyed the negative thrill of a dialogue with the Devil. Again, as in the case of the boys' mother, this dialogue acted as a provocation and thus brought forth the worst in the possessing entity and its human vehicles.

With possession lasting for four years, the period occupied a major portion in the two boys' lives. For Theobald, possession took up the period when he was between ten and fourteen years of age. He did not live much longer. The Illfurth records show that Theobald Bruner died on April 3, 1871, at the age of sixteen. His younger brother, Joseph, whose possession would seem to have been a less virulent one, and perhaps something of an echo of Theobald's experience, lived longer. He was twenty-five years old when he died, in 1882.

The Illfurth case, for all its gaps—notably concerning the Bruner's family history prior to the possession—is one of the best documented in recent history. In addition to the record compiled by Father Brey, a report by the bishop's commission on this case was filed, and written accounts provided by various local authorities complete the narrative. A modern summary of the case was published in Germany in 1954 by Peter Sutter under the title *Satans Macht und Wirken* (*Satan's Power and Influence*).

Ecclesiastical authorities on possession and exorcism emphasize that the Devil uses weaknesses inherent in each individual to achieve his aim: the possession and, if possible, destruction of the person. Among those who have been mentioned as most vulnerable to diabolical manipulation are men or women who tend toward mental depression or emotional violence. Whether possession in the strict ecclesiastical sense is involved, or what some Catholic psychologists have termed "pseudopossession," psychological stress factors existed in the Bruner family. Modern Church authorities might not agree with their nineteenth-century counterparts, who classified the Illfurth boys as definitely Devil-possessed.

It may be assumed that both boys, but the older Theobald more so than the younger Joseph, were in a stage of preadolescent rebellion against their parents and the restrictions of an obviously strict religious upbringing. Their mother, Mrs. Bruner, would seem to have been horrified as well as fascinated by her boys' diabolical possession. Her position as target and guardian of the boys, the notoriety and attention that possession brought the Bruner family, might well have prompted the mother to play a central and at times provocative role with a certain degree of ardor.

The Illfurth records virtually ignore the boys' father, who may well have wondered about the nature and origin of the possession phenomena, but could easily have been prompted into silent agreement by the formidable alliance of his wife with the local priest, Father Brey, and with high-level ecclesiastical authorities.

Theobald's fate, his death two years after the end of the exorcism, is a tragic one. Modern psychosomatic medicine could easily speculate that *anorexia nervosa* (serious malnutrition based on emotional factors), which is relatively frequent in adolescents, may have seriously weakened the boy. The term conversion hysteria, which is often applied to cases that show symptoms similar to those in the Illfurth case, might also be applied.

Yet, in the time and place in which young Theobald and Joseph went through their four years of suffering and horror, Devil possession was the appropriate diagnosis, and exorcism the obvious means of achieving a cure. Regrettably, at least in the Theobald's case, the cure was short-lived. We can only look back on the case, humbly and prayerfully.

15. Conception of the Demon Child

Jules-Sylvestre Diamant

This exploration into origins of the demon-child image uses the word "conception" in a dual sense: the ideological roots of the "demon child" term, and the sexual conception of such a child by a demonic entity through the body of a human female. Dr. Diamant, who lives near Lyons, France, is a frequent contributor to folkloric and parapsychological publications. Here, he links sixteenth-century traditions with modern research and physics, as well as with non-European ideas that parallel the occult-religious concept of intercourse with such other-worldly entities as an incubus (male) or succubus (female).

Demoniality was originally defined by Ludovico Sinistrari, onetime Vicar General to the Archbishop of Avignon and professor of philosophy at Pavia, as a *congressus cum daemone*—specifically, sexual intercourse with an infernal spirit.

Such intercourse could result in offspring, they being characterized by certain qualities which we will take up in their place. However, Sinistrari's greatest contribution was to define and delineate the true nature of the extrahuman entity involved in the liaison.

Sinistrari wrote in *Of Demoniality, the Incubus and the Succubus (De Demonialitate et incubus et succubus)* at the end of the seventeenth century. The exact date is not known since the manuscript was lost. It turned up, by accident, among some trivia in a London bookseller's stall in 1872 and was finally published in 1875.

Certainly in all the time the manuscript was lost it could

not receive the scholarly comment and criticism it deserved. Nor is it our purpose to take up that task in these pages. We are concerned here with the occult and sexual aspects of coitus with an extrahuman entity and with the nature of the offspring to be expected therefrom.

That a nubile woman could have sexual intercourse with a demon and conceive from it is a tradition that goes back so far as to be lost in letterless antiquity. We know, not only from the Biblical *Genesis*, but from the apocryphal *I Enoch*, the story of the Watchers, the sleepless angels, the Children of Heaven, who looked upon human womankind and "saw and lusted after them, and said to one another, 'Come, let us choose wives from among these children of men and beget us children . . . And they took wives and began to go into them and defile themselves with them . . . "

The offspring were giants who ate up all the possessions of men. "And when men could no longer sustain them, the giants turned against them and they devoured mankind, and they began to sin against birds and beasts and reptiles and fish, and to devour one another's flesh and to drink the blood . . ." The good God sent the Archangel Michael to bind the giants in the valleys of the earth until the day of judgment when they could be rendered unto the jaws of Hell. But, out of the dead bodies of the giants rose demons who, ever since, have been the cause of wickedness, oppression, destruction, and the most diabolical seductions and rapes.

It is surprising to find the same tale told in South American traditions—of giants who built the Andes city of Tiahuanaco. Those giants seized the women of men but rent and killed them, because their members were so huge. Then they turned homosexual and died out, leaving only their evil spirits behind them.

Commentators upon the Old Testament have advanced a theory that finds a parallel in modern occult lore. It is said that, before Eve, Adam had a wife named Lilith. But, say the scholars, Lilith was only a product of Adam's sexual fantasies. His seed, released by masturbation or nocturnal emission, could impregnate no phantom Lilith, but, falling on the ground, would have given rise to demons who would have had none but a fantasy mother.

The American occultist, L. W. de Laurence of Chicago, has pointed out that the human mind, when excited to lewd imagination or lustful phantasy, generates an astral sperm on another plane from this. From that astral sperm, the lascivious *incubi* and *succubi* arise.

Prominent authorities such as Albertus Magnus and Thomas Aquinas, his pupil, saw an incubus as an extrahuman entity manifesting itself in the form of a human male in order to effect sexual intercourse with a woman. The entity of itself had no sex. The succubus is such an entity manifesting as a woman in order to lie under a man.

Prominent authorities such as Albertus Magnus and his pupil, Thomas Aquinas, conceived of impregnation as occurring in this way. A spirit, as succubus, would couple with a man, drawing all his seed into itself. Then, manifesting as an incubus, the male form would penetrate a woman and flood her womb with the stolen seed.

Sinistrari took exception to this. He pointed out that there was a species of extrahuman being that possessed a very subtle material nature and demonstrated that such a being would have a sexual nature and appetite. It would be either male or female. As a male, it would ejaculate its own seed into the woman to her embarrassment or disgrace. The female would drain the male to the point of impotency through vaginal intercourse or fellatio, rendering him incapable of meeting the marital requirements of his wife.

Drawing upon some very powerful philosophical authority, Sinistrari cited both Plato and Plutarch to show that the extra-corporeal entities he referred to were, like man, beings of the animal kind, with rational intelligences and aerial bodies composed of matter in a very rarefied form. This strikes a familiar note to the occult psychologist.

What Sinistrari describes in his text *is not a spiritual being.* It is a being composed of matter, like man, but as dense as flesh. This being we can identify because Sinistrari relates them to the primal elements of Fire, Earth, Air, and Water. He is talking about *Elementals.*

Once we understand that, then the behavior of the entity becomes clear. Elementals, according to occult theory, are soulless beings which have a spiritual consciousness more keen than man's though their intelligence falls somewhat below his. (Psychologists of a certain school would say they're more of the *feeling* than the *thinking* type.) In some respects, though, particularly in view of the fact that they are not so heavily burdened with material substance as he is.

Occult theory teaches that the Elementals were made to

serve man, but that he abused them, and thereby incurred their dumb but dogged enmity. Thus they are hostile to man and seek to achieve his confusion and downfall. This does much to explain the japes of the so-called demon lover. When an Elemental assumes the role of incubus, two roads are open to him. He may vent his lust on women who offer themselves to him in such occult services as the witches' sabbath or the Black Mass. Or, he may take a more circuitous route and try to seduce her by various underhand methods. These may range all the way from simply taking the likeness of her husband in bed, or inundating her with all sorts of expensive gifts and lavish favors until she succumbs to his lust.

The woman who is seduced has the best of the two alternatives. To her the incubus is a lover of more than human skill, with a rare wisdom of penetration and rhythm and a supernal stamina. Despite this, he may treat her cruelly at times. One tale tells of an incubus who caused all the clothing and jewelry to vanish away from the lady to whom he had given them, leaving her completely naked in the midst of a crowded church. Another materialized in the guise of a (real) handsome village youth in a husband's presence, and then ran from the woman, leaving her to be beaten by her angered spouse. Others, upon the approach of witnesses, have rendered themselves invisible while still in the sexual act, causing the onlookers to believe the woman was bereft of her senses.

With those who offer themselves to him voluntarily at occult services, the incubus is apt to express his hostility and contempt through hideous brutalities. His oversize member becomes like a bruising bar of iron and may be as cold as ice or hot as fire. It may be feathered with scales that cruelly tear vaginal flesh as it is withdrawn. His victims find themselves powerless and incapable of any defense. He may brutalize every orifice of their bodies, leering and deaf to their shrieks and pleas.

In those rare cases where the woman he has seduced arouses no sadistic instincts she may find she has. R. E. L. Masters, in his *Eros and Evil*, finds that no surprise should be occasioned by the concept of an incubus as the ideal lover, capable of fulfilling the most intense unconscious as well as conscious cravings of women. He says: "With him, since at the first embrace, one has given oneself over completely to evil and damnation, all restraints may be cast aside, all cravings indulged. There is nothing more to lose, so all becomes permissible . . . . What a woman does with her incubus may be what she would wish to do with her man—if she were not a good woman, if she were not afraid, if repression and suppression did not frustrate and inhibit her."

Unpredictably, though, the incubus may murder his mistress. His usual way is to kill her by breaking her neck, twisting it so forcibly that the slain victim is found with her head facing backwards. Sinistrari points out that this is no evil on the part of the incubus; for, being superior to man, he may kill a human being just as man kills the animals and fowl of the fields for his own purposes.

The incubus may or may not cause conception to occur. If he does, for reasons of his own, he is well prepared to do so, according to Thomas Malvenda, a Spanish physician of the sixteenth century. Malvenda wrote: "What incubi introduce into the womb is not any ordinary human semen in normal quantity, but abundant, very thick, very warm, rich in spirits and free from serosity . . . taking care that both shall enjoy a more than normal orgasm, for the more abundant is the semen the greater is the venereal excitement."

Jerome Cardano, occultist and mathematician of the seventeenth century, believed that incubi only appeared handsome to the woman he lay with; to others he appeared in a less gracious form. A lovely young woman, wrote Cardano, confessed to her parents that she was pregnant. She said her lover was a handsome youth who would appear suddenly in her room, take her to bed, and as mysteriously disappear. The parents decided to look into her room at night. They saw her in the extremest sexual throes with a hideous monster. Having come prepared, they read an exorcism ritual and the great scaly beast flapped away on leathery wings, setting the house on fire as he went. The girl, in her time, gave birth to a monster that the authorities shudderingly destroyed in a great bonfire. But the girl would never admit to seeing the incubus as other than a beautiful youth.

Yet, in another work, Sinistrari tells a different story. In his *De Delictis et Poenis* (roughly, "Crime and Punishment") we find strange doings in a convent. In her cell, a nun hears sounds of thumping and bed-squeaking and passionate moans from the next room. The nun who lives there comes out alone and the room is found to be empty upon inspection. Finally, having bored a small hole in the wall, the abbess, the first nun, and a couple of witnesses, saw a "comely youth" making love to the nun next door. But, when they forced the door of the next room, they found its occupant alone. She confessed, however, to having entertained an incubus.

Thus the testimony must be seen as divided on how an incubus is seen by onlookers; but it may be that this is something depending upon individual incubic whim. Sinistrari made an important point with regard to that anecdote, however. *If* the nun had called up the incubus by heretical ritual, she was guilty of a crime against religion; if she merely succumbed to the seduction of an incubus who has come of his own accord, she sinned only against chastity.

There is no predicting the form that offspring of a demon may take. The fetus may grow to immense proportions within the womb. In Herefordshire, England, in 1249, a woman delivered a child that grew to the height of a man within months. In another case, in 1336, a fetus of prodigious size was carried by another woman. She died before she could give birth to it. Eight strong men had to carry her to her grave. At Esslingen, Germany, in 1545, an incubus wrought a hideous pregnancy upon a girl named Margaret. Her abdomen grew so large that attendants could not see her face or feet. From within her came the most horrible roarings and howlings, and finally she bore all kinds of loathsome creatures.

When the fetus approached pathological normalcy, there was usually a critical period which began at birth. In many cases, the infant was stillborn. If it lived, it was stunted, wizened, and discolored. Though they are smaller in size, they have a greater weight than other children, as if somehow they were made of a much denser substance. If the incubus child survives birth, he may soon disappear in a mysterious way. The assumption is that he has been carried off by the incubus or the devil, or that he may only have been an *effigy*, a simulacrum of an infant having only a tentative quality of reality that evaporates of itself in time. This may happen from one to six weeks after birth.

If the infant is not carried away by supernal means, the next critical period begins about the seventh year. Between birth and that time, the child shows unpleasant character traits—constant bawling, demanding inordinate amounts of food and milk, a mocking laughter when the household is afflicted by troubles, and a most contemptible meanness toward other children and small animals.

If the second critical period is survived, the child begins to grow at a great rate, soon outstripping neighboring children in height, weight, hardiness, and athletic ability. They become very grave and aggressive and seem to draw upon some inner sources of knowledge that elude the most persistent fathoming.

Many of history's great men are said to have been fathered by incubi. This includes the philosopher Plato. Alexander the Great and Caesar Augustus had incubus parents, it is said; so did Seleucus, King of Persia. The mysterious figure known as Malkin or Merlin was sired by an incubus upon a nun who was Charlemagne's daughter. There are many, many more.

Today we are in the midst of revising much of our scientific thinking. We have found that our cosmos partakes more of the nature of insubstantial thought than it does of matter—according to some Nobel Prize-winning physicists—and some have gone so far as to assert that such a physical but nonmaterial universe could be manipulated by nonmaterial thought.

This gives us an uneasy insight into what may be the real nature of the incubus, one that is in some agreement with the occult principle, already mentioned, that was enunciated by L. W. de Laurence, that the mode of incubus creation lies in the unchecked lustfulness of the imagination. This would equate the incubus with the "tulpa" of *The Tibetan Book of the Dead*, or a thought-form creation like the dread *Egrigor*. And suggests more than casual heed might be given to the line from Thomas Mann's *Faust*: "Who believes in the Devil, belongs to him already."

16. Salem's Children

Anthony Garrett

The very term "Witches of Salem" has become standard in American history of Colonial times. Historians have, for the most part, concentrated on the charges, trials, and burnings of the adult "witches" accused in this Massachusetts cauldron of events. But what, precisely, was the role of the Salem children? Isn't it true that the whole frightful chain of events was begun by Salem's children? And what evil, demonic, or possessing force may have been at work in using these children as a force in the chaos, fear, and hate that struck the New England community? Mr. Garrett, who explores these questions, is a free-lance journalist and author of several essays on early New England history. He attended Clark University, Worcester, Massachusetts and has worked on several newspapers. At present he is preparing a study of H. P. Lovecraft: The Man and His Sources. He lives with his family near Seekonk, Rhode Island.

In 1697, the Inferior Court of Common Pleas, Massachusetts Province, Dominion of New England, ruled that the Reverend Samuel Parris, minister, be separated from his church in Salem Village. Effectively, this was a dismissal from the area as well, for Parris had no occupation other than his calling and the villagers flatly refused to hear his ministry in any church at all.

This seems like one of the many other downbeat endings following the Salem witchcraft scandal, particularly since Parris appears from the beginning to have been an aggrieved person. It was his nine-year-old daughter, Elizabeth, who was the first person to be afflicted. When Doctor of Medicine

William Griggs diagnosed her problem as the result of witchcraft, Parris refused to believe it. It was some nosy soup-carrying neighbors who took up the witchcraft cry. Thus dismissal does not seem like justice to an innocent and troubled father.

But there was probably just as much valid evidence ignored in the Salem trials as there was in the assassination of President John F. Kennedy, and, though a review of the trials may lead to conclusions distasteful to overemotional types who fall to their knees as if in worship at the sound of the word *children*; still, in the Salem of 1692, a dread aura of evil seems to hang like a noxious fog around at least one of the "children" said to be afflicted.

Little Elizabeth Parris seems to have been completely guiltless. She wasn't even in Salem Village when the trouble started. Her father had spirited her away to stay at the home of Stephen Sewall in Salem Town. (I should caution here against the common error of confusing the Salem of today with Salem Village. It was Salem Village—which quickly changed its name to Danvers, the one it has now, where the witchcraft activity occurred. Tourists who try to tune in to bad vibes in modern Salem are five miles off course.)

At the instigation of a playmate, eleven-year-old Abigail Williams, Elizabeth Parris got involved in a petty occult scam. It consisted in dropping the white of eggs into a glass and concentrating upon the goo to see if she could learn something of her future husband.

The specter of a coffin appeared and Elizabeth went into a fit.

This parlor witchcraft has been laid to Tituba, servant to the Reverend Samuel, who baby-sat the two girls. Tituba, whom popular error insists on making a black woman instead of the West Indian woman she was, is slighted here. If Tituba had taught the girls any occultery, it would have been in the light of her own culture.

Assuming that Elizabeth was too young to have knowledge of the scrying technique, even though it is standard in English witchcraft, we can lay the suggestion of the game to young Abigail Williams.

Now any professional historian, in his superficial and selective reading of the Salem evidence, would be unable to escape the conclusion that Abigail was one of those snot-nosed kids best coped with by a vehement blow with a cast-iron skillet. Still, something darker than mere brattish viciousness looms here.

With Elizabeth five miles out of the way in the Sewall household, we suddenly find that others, including Abigail, begin to show symptoms diagnosed by Dr. Griggs as the effects of witchcraft. They were not all little girls, either: Mary Warren was twenty years old; Mercy Lewis, nineteen; Elizabeth Hubbard, seventeen; and Mary Walcott, sixteen. It is Mary Walcott who bids for our attention next: she and Abigail Williams seem to have worked with the precision and finesse of a well-rehearsed theatrical team.

We find them concentrating on the Reverend Deodat Lawson. He had come to Salem Village because the girls claimed his wife and daughter, who were buried there, had been killed by witchcraft. When Lawson came to the Village, he put up at Ingersoll's Tavern. Sixteen-year-old Mary Walcott came to the common room. After a time, and in front of the assembled company, she let out a shrill scream. Do-gooders slavered by her side until, to their horror and delight, they saw the marks of teeth, "both upper and lower set," appear upon her arm.

Whether this was rather much for the Reverend Deodat, he did not indicate; but he did saunter over to Parris' parsonage. Abigail Williams was there. She immediately favored him with what he described as "a grievous fit."

The next day, as visiting minister, Lawson preached a sermon. The girls were there. "They had several sore fits in the time of public worship, which did something interrupt me in my first prayer, being so unusual," he lamented. The sermon was to come next, but before it could begin, the nasty voice of Abigail sang out, "Now stand up and name your text!"

Disconcerted at the crudeness, Lawson said he would speak on, "Christ's Fidelity the Only Shield Against Satan's Malignity."

Called out Abigail, "That's a long text!"

Martha Corey, one of the witch suspects accused by the girls of causing their afflictions attended the sermon. Abigail called out, "Look where Goodwife Corey sits on the beam, suckling her yellow bird!"

She referred to an apparition of Goodwife Corey, supposedly nursing her witches' familiar in the form of a bird.

This was Abigail's favorite ploy, to say that she saw someone's apparition hovering in an assembly. It is noteworthy that it was she who saw the apparition first, and only secondly did others of the afflicted take up the cry. This is particularly marked in the trial of Elizabeth Procter who, Abigail claimed, had appeared to her as an apparition and asked her to sign a book. Abigail alleged that Mrs. Procter had said that Mary Warren, another of the afflicted, had already signed it. (Procter: "Dear child, it is not so. There is another judgment, dear child.")

Abigail screeched that she saw Elizabeth Procter's apparition seated above the spectators on a beam. The other afflicted took up the cry. Then Abigail whinnied, "There goes [the apparition of] John Procter! He is going to Mrs. Pope!" Mrs. Pope had a fit. Abigail: "There is John Procter going to hurt Mrs. Bibber!" Mrs. Bibber had a fit, too.

Abigail's incrimination of John Procter caused him to be cited along with his wife. Both were found guilty and sentenced to death by the special Court of Oyer and Terminer the absent Governor Phips had convened. Elizabeth "pleaded her belly": a pregnant woman could not be executed; John was hanged on August 19.

Once Abigail—or it could have been Mary Walcott; the testimony is ambiguous—while at Ingersoll's Tavern during a conversation on the Procter examination, cried out, "There's Mrs. Procter! There's Mrs. Procter! Old witch, I'll have her hanged!"

A certain William Raymond who was there called the girl a liar and said he saw nothing. Mrs. Ingersoll joined in and berated the girl. The girl, Abigail or Mary, then backed down and tried to make a joke of the whole thing, saying she only did it for sport; she had to have some sport.

Six men and fourteen women died as the result of the witchcraft investigation. Not to mention five-year-old Dorcas Good. Little Dorcas, whose fortitude was not up to being chained in the dark depths of Boston gaol's dungeon, came down with a permanent case of insanity.

That's a fine crop of gallows' fruit to be sown and reaped by a human child. But: *was Abigail Williams a human child?*

Anyone who reads the witchcraft trial records and their contemporaneous commentaries must conclude that there was a lot more going on in Salem Village than met the eye—or that a good deal of testimony to a dark reign of diabolism has been carefully suppressed.

The affliction of Elizabeth Parris began in March. At that time, Governor William Phips and Increase Mather—Cotton's father—were in England negotiating a new colonial charter. They did not get back to Boston until May 14, 1692. By this time over one hundred defendants from Salem had been lodged in Boston jail. This represented a potential one hundred death sentences and certainly a great sociopolitical crisis, an emergency that would seem to demand the constant presence of the governor. Yet, Governor Phips made haste to get out of town with a body of militia, on the pretext of fighting the French and Indians—despite the fact that they posed no threat to Massachusetts at the time.

The trials would ordinarily have been handled by the Supreme Court of Judicature. But Phips did not convene the Court. Instead, he ordered a special Court of Oyer and Terminer and staffed it himself with handpicked men. In spite of the fact that seventeenth-century judicial procedure was fairly enlightened—in other witchcraft cases the accused were given what amounted to psychiatric examinations "to see if They be crazed in their Intellectuals"—and, in spite of the fact that Cotton Mather constantly protested its conduct of the trial, the Oyer and Terminer bench carried on in the traditions of the Spanish Inquisition.

It is clear that the Oyer and Terminer Court was determined to wipe out something and to wipe it out with a vehemence that knew no mercy. But this being so, we are confronted with a surprising mystery: Not one of the accused who confessed to witchcraft was executed, much less brought to trial!

In other words, there was a jail full of people who were self-confessed perpetrators of a crime that carried a mandatory death sentence, and the Oyer and Terminer Court treated them as if they didn't exist. Then what was Oyer and Terminer after?

The Oyer and Terminer trials have obscured the fact that witchcraft was not confined to Salem. There were trials in Boston, Hartford, Groton, Northhampton, Hadley, and Springfield, too. So witchcraft was not exactly a rarity in New England, despite the fact that, not counting Salem, less than thirty people had ever been hanged for it in the entire seventeenth century.

Here and there, throughout the historical records of the period, we find references that show the practice of witch-

craft was not restricted to the country folk. There is plenty of
evidence that many of the upper class were involved. In one
confession, we hear of a meeting of 105 young men, "some
with rapiers by their sides" (i.e., gentlemen), assembling for
a satanic sacrament near the meeting house of Salem Village.
We find mention of an admitted witch appearing in company
with "a lady from Boston." We know the annual baptism of
new witches was at Five Mile Pond in Fall River and that it
included "many that were of the quality."

And, had not the trial been called off, at a subsequent
session, Governor Phips' wife was to be named among some
other prominent Bostonians, according to Robert Calef's eye-
witness reportage of the trials and executions. No wonder
Phips found reason to get out of town!

One would have thought that in the period of insight and
awakening, of penitence and self-recrimination that followed
the trials, the judges who had served on the Court of Oyer
and Terminer would have suffered the judgment of a shocked
public. Not at all. They were rewarded, instead. At the next
polling, every single one of them was elected to the Governor's Council.

On September 22, 1692 Cotton Mather met with some of
the trial judges to discuss his forthcoming book on the cases.
Whatever he was told there, he made no record of it, but he
left the meeting a newly informed man—and abandoned his
previous criticism of the court to become its staunchest de-
fender!

Out of this welter of mysteries surrounding the most famous witchcraft trials in history, a faint hint of a solution
seems to rise and beg for recognition. Suppose, for example,
that witchcraft of a sort represented an exciting underground
way of life in the seventeenth century. We have a parallel in
our own times, when uncountable thousands of affluent,
well-educated people light a joint of pot with one hand and
thumb their noses at law and convention with the other.

And suppose that, out of that illegal but accepted order of
witchcraft, something darker arose, something that proper
Bostonians and sedulous Salemites had not given a thought
to. Say, that in the darker rites of witchcraft, sexual copu-
lation with a demon occurs as a matter of course. This is not
something that would necessarily be practiced in Boston; in
fact the Bostonians might have regarded it as an amusing
provincialism.

Until the children started to come.

How many demon children were spawned in those dark Massachusetts forests is anyone's guess. But the authorities, knowing something was wrongly out of line with the witchcraft game they had winked at before, were ready to accept any testimony at all that innocent people were really the evilest kind of diabolists.

They believed the demon children were pointing out to them the people who practiced the wrong kind of witchcraft. And they conspired to liquidate those people.

All to the glee of the demon children.

Records are silent as to the fate of Abigail Williams. A book published in 1702 speaks of her as if she were already dead. It mentions that, wherever she went during the rest of her short life, she was attended "by diabolical manifestations."

How did she die? We can only conjecture. But it's an odds-on bet her body was buried at a crossroads.

And, as for our friend, the Reverend Mr. Parris, we might never have known the real complaint that Salem Village had against him, except for the brief mention in the records of the Inferior Court of Common Pleas, of his "going to Mary Walcott or Abigail Williams and directing others to them," that Parris had been "the beginner and procurer of the sorest afflictions, not to this village only but to this whole country, that did ever befall them . . ."

17. The Possession of Germana

Pamela White

Demon possession is universal. It is widely experienced, and countered by exorcisms, in various parts of the African continent and in several regions of the Near and Far East. In Latin America, African traditions have been adapted to local religiocultural conditions. Specifically in Brazil and Haiti, Roman Catholic concepts can be found in conjunction with African beliefs and practices. The unique case presented in the following pages deals with a similar interaction between African and Christian traditions, as observed in a teen-age girl at a South African missionary post.

Germana came to the Roman Catholic missionary station of the Marianhill Order when she was only four years old. She remained at the mission all her life; when she was about sixteen, she announced that she had made a pact with the Devil and showed numerous possession symptoms. The station was located in the town of Umzinto, some fifty miles from Durban, Natal, South Africa. Germana was born in 1890, and her exorcism took place, with interruptions, during 1906 and 1907. Among the outstanding features of the possession was Germana's great physical strength while under demonic or diabolical control. She battered those who tried to control her, and she promised vengeance to her guards. Early on, when two nuns expressed the view that she was faking demon control, Germana warned, "I'll deal with them, so they'll never forget it." The nuns had been asked by the station's mother superior to guard the girl.

As related by Father Erasmus Hörner, Germana's exorcist, the two nuns were accompanied by three hefty assistants when they came to guard her one evening. In the beginning, the girl was affable. Germana chatted with her guards and seemed in a good mood. But soon she began to ask "tricky questions," apparently of a theological nature, and an argument started. Father Hörner wrote that "before anyone realized what was going on, Germana stood before the sisters in blazing anger and upbraided them in a manner they would always remember for its lack of devotion and grace." This is what happened next:

"When they made moves as if they might hit her, Germana streaked for the door like lightning, locked it, and put the key in her pocket. Then she grabbed the two nuns by their caps, shook them and, with a giant's strength, slammed one into one corner and threw the second into another corner of the room. Germana then severely beat one sister, tore the veil from her head, and left her in a daze; with that, she pushed her with a sudden move under the bed. With equal speed, she was on top of the other nun, who was crouching in a corner, choked and beat her. Next, she beat every one of them in turn. Of the three girls, none tried to touch her during this condition."

The contemporary German exorcism authority, Father Adolf Rodewyk, a Jesuit priest and diocesan consultant, has observed that Germana developed unusual strength while under diabolic control, but also showed how quickly a crisis condition can develop, even right in the middle of a conversation. On the surface, he noted, Germana "simply got angry," but "such strong emotional reactions are often mere camouflage for a crisis condition; apparently natural anger may serve as a bridge into the actual possession stage."

Writing in his book, *Possessed by Satan* (New York 1975), Rodewyk said that a possession stage could have been confirmed later on, "if it had been found that amnesia existed." He added: "It was only necessary to inquire what the girl actually remembered afterward; this would have made it possible to determine, up to the second, just when the Devil had taken over. Such trance conditions contain nothing of the slowness or even sleeplike condition of the mediumistic trance. Germana acted quickly, as if executing a tactically conceived plan."

A second incident served to explain Germana's condition. While she was in a severe possession crisis, raving and acting destructively, a young priest came to perform an exorcism. In accordance with the instructions of the sixteenth-century *Rituale Romanum*, he wore a stole and began praying. He was soon interrupted by a voice speaking through Germana. When the priest asked the diabolic voice to be quiet, the girl became even more violent. Forgetting himself, the young priest slapped Germana, who yelled at him: "Why do you beat me? You know full well that it isn't I, Germana, who is doing this, but the one who is within me. Does one beat a spirit? Is that what a priest does?"

When the young priest, impatiently, sought to slap her again, Germana knocked the volume of the exorcism rite out of his hand, and in quick movements tore the stole from his neck, tore it to ribbons, grabbed the man by his neck, choked him, and threw him to the ground. The priest sought to fight back, and it was quite a battle. Germana, or the diabolic spirit within her, was stronger, and she shoved the priest under the bed. He was hurt; his fingers were badly bruised, and his body was covered with scratches and abrasions. Now, Germana began to weep. She was sitting in a corner of the room, apparently disconsolate, when others came to see what the commotion had been about.

Rodewyk comments on this incident by saying that Germana came to her senses, after the Devil within her had made her beat the priest. He adds: "The struggle symbolized more than just a display of great strength. It helps to clarify the matter. We learn who is behind all this, that one cannot confront the Devil during a possession crisis with pride and self-assertion, or he will let the human being feel who he really is. Possessed persons can be quite dangerous!" It is obviously extremely difficult to an outside observer, or even the exorcist himself, to tell the difference between the person who is possessed and the entity within the person. Germana seems to have been a girl of considerable physical strength on her own, but showed superhuman strength while in an overt state of diabolical possession.

One highly unusual phenomenon, rarely observed outside mediumistic circles or the field of stage magic, is that of levitation. It falls into the category of supernatural capabilities that are symptoms of possessions by the Devil, demons or evil spirits. In the Germana case, Father Hörner reports the following phenomena:

"Germana floated often three, four, and up to five feet in the air, sometimes vertically, with her feet downward, and at other times horizontally, with her whole body floating above her bed. She was in a rigid position. Even her clothing did not fall downward, as would have been normal; instead, her dresses remained tightly attached to her body and legs. If she was sprinkled with holy water, she moved down immediately, and her clothing fell loosely onto her bed. This type of the phenomenon took place in the presence of witnesses, including outsiders. Even in church, where she could be seen by everyone, she floated above her seat. Some people tried to pull her down forcibly, holding on to her feet, but it proved to be impossible."

One should not get the impression, from this mental picture, that Germana was in a state of relaxation while she levitated above the ground. On the contrary, levitation occurred during periods of such physical and verbal violence that she often had to have her hands tied to keep her from destroying property or harming others. One such incident illustrates the effort needed to keep the girl under control:

"Everyone sought to help, but it still took another three hours before we were finally able to put handcuffs on the girl, as she was in a state of violent anger. Both her arms were stiff and immovable. At the same time, and amid horrible noise and disturbance, she was, over and over again, levitated off the ground while sitting in her chair."

Rodewyk cites this scene as illustrating vividly that the exorcist was dealing with "extraordinary powers of strength," indicating true diabolic or demon possession. He added: "We should keep in mind that some sixteen persons were trying to hold Germana and tie her up. Needless to say, we are not, in such instances, dealing with the spiritual and physical uplift we encounter during mystical ecstasy!"

Mysterious fire phenomena also occurred in Germana's presence. Once, when she entered a kitchen where a small coal fire was glowing, a huge flame suddenly shot into the air. While others cried out and fled, Germana laughed and moved away slowly. The room was filled with flames, although only a few half-glowing bits of coal remained in the kitchen ashes. Another fire phenomenon took place when the girls were going to bed and while Germana was surrounded by twenty other girls to the left and right of her. The girls had just retired and the room supervisor, Sister Juliana was resting in a deck chair, when Germana's bed began to creak and shake. Next, flames shot up from her bed. They subsided when Sister Juliana sprinkled holy water on the bed. When the bed was later examined, the possibility that Germana might have set fire to it herself was ruled out: bedposts and boards were half-burned but the girl's covers and clothing remained unsinged.

Around the girl, infestations by unexplained noises—phenomena associated with poltergeist cases throughout the world—were noted. These upset the other girls in the mission station greatly, and Father Erasmus Hörner, the exorcist, was agitated by the restlessness and confusion they created. Often, during the night, loud poundings could be heard at the door leading into the house in which the girls slept. Hörner and another priest armed themselves and began to guard the house, thinking that an outsider hostile to the mission might be involved and was endangering the girls' peace of mind.

The two priests occupied an empty room close to the sleeping quarters of the girls. When they began their vigil, everything was quiet. But not for long. Hörner reported on the events that followed:

"Suddenly, at ten o'clock, there was a sound like a thunderclap at the door. Inside, everyone cried out in fear and horror. We hurried outside, to find out what was going on. Then, once again, one, two, five tremendous blows. We went out once more, and again there was nothing in sight. Banging and pounding could be heard on several doors inside the house. We went to investigate and found nothing. The noise and pounding continued in the rooms of the brothers [monks and priests], in the smithy, in the storage section, and even in the shed where the animals had become restless, but nowhere was anything to be seen. The noise stopped by eleven-fifteen.

"During the day on which these phenomena occurred, Germana seemed oddly amused and laughed a great deal. The next day Sister Juliana had this to say: 'Last night around nine Germana suddenly began laughing and said: "Just now the pastor and his brother are going downstairs to stand guard. He even has a gun with him. As if he could shoot a ghost with a gun! Is the Father really that stupid? I'm sorry for the poor father, who gives so much help to me and others, but the one who is inside me is only taking a grim delight and pleasure in all this." ' "

The possession began when Germana confessed to a pact with the Devil. On July 5, 1906, she handed Father Hörner, who had acted as her confessor, a sheet of paper on which she had written the text of a Satanic pact. She also acted violently and cried out, "I am lost! I have confessed and taken Communion under false pretenses! I must hang myself; Satan is calling me." The following month, on August 20, she had what looked like a hysterical fit: Germana tore her dress to pieces, broke the post of her bed, ground her teeth, growled and barked like a dog, grunted like a pig, and called Juliana for help: "Sister, please call Father Erasmus. I must confess and tell everything. But be quick, quick, or Satan will kill me. He has me in his power! Nothing blessed is with me; I have thrown away all the medals you have given me."

Later that day, she seemed to be arguing with invisible entities. She would ask or answer questions, and when she did so, her head was suddenly pulled to the left. It seemed to the other girls that she was fighting with the Devil. They recalled that she said, at one point, "You have betrayed me. You have promised me days of glory, but now you treat me cruelly."

While she was engaged in this argument with the Invisible, the girl was shoved against the wall, as if by a strong hand. One of the nuns urged Germana to fight the diabolic force by renewing her baptismal pledge. The girl seemed to make an effort to form the words of the pledge, but only uttered a few words. Instead of completing it, she stopped when she came to the phrase ". . . and to Jesus Christ." Instead, she shouted, "No, never! That is why we are what we are. We never refused our adoration of the Son, but withheld it from the man—no, never!" After this, the possession symptoms increased and the diabolic presence was soon clearly felt.

The Devil's voice was, from then on, repeatedly and clearly heard coming from Germana's lips. Father Hörner particularly noted that the Devil clearly suggested he was possessing the girl with God's permission, a point that has a strong theological significance. Satan, according to this view, can only act as far and as long as God unleashes him. At one point, during church services, Germana placed herself before the open tabernacle, and the diabolical voice said through her, "I swear before God, whom I hate and who is present in this sacrament, that he permitted me to enter Germana. There is Jesus, who permitted me to enter Germana."

The girl turned to open rebellion during religious services. She disrupted sermons, stuck out her tongue defiantly, and once shouted at the priest, "Stop preaching, you torture me." When holy water was sprinkled on her, she complained that it burned her skin. Once, plain water was substituted for holy water in the fount; but when it was sprinkled on her, she immediately knew the difference, and just laughed about the attempted trick. Yet, when the fount was switched back to holy water, she said, "Stop, it burns!"

She reacted similarly to other ecclesiastical elements. Germana could tell holy water from plain water also when it was given to her to drink. When a blessed stole was put on her, she shouted, "Take it away. It is heavy and oppressive." Like other possessed people, she reacted violently and specifically to the cross. She could recognize a cross even though she had been handed only fragments of one, wrapped carefully and securely.

Father Hörner's report stated that Germana was able to recognize consecrated medals and said that the Devil was frustrated in his efforts to control her, as long as holy items were near her or were being worn by her. The different reaction to consecrated and unconsecrated items even extended to persons. When she shouted loudly and a bishop placed his two consecrated fingers at her throat, Germana immediately fell silent. But when, on a similar occasion, a nun tried to do the same thing, it didn't work. When she was asked, what had made the difference, the girl said about the priest, "Because his hands have been anointed."

Because the girl alternated between states of diabolical possession and her own normal state, she was able to undergo confession and take Communion during the whole possession period. This, however, involved physical and spiritual risks, of which Father Hörner became quickly aware. She often asked him to hear her confessions, just to have peace from the Devil. Father Hörner described his dilemma as follows:

"Often, hearing her confess was a difficult task, a trial of human patience. A dual problem was faced. At times, one could not be sure whether it was Germana or the demon who spoke. In several instances, a self-dialogue seemed to be going on. It was if two beings were speaking through Germana's mouth. Once, the young girl said, 'But I am telling Father everything; I am fed up with you; you are pressing me too hard. Is that what I deserve? I confess in order to be free of you.' The confession, after some hesitation, continued. In another instance, the girl was unable to speak, as if her throat had been closed."

Father Hörner also noted that he had to be very careful

during Holy Communion, as "Satan tempted her constantly."
Germana seemed "forever tempted to pull the holy items
from her mouth, to spit them out, or to degrade them in
some manner." He added:

"At times, she was unable to swallow altogether, or only
with great difficulty. She gagged and strained, but the back of
her mouth remained rigid. When I placed the two anointed
priestly fingers on her neck, the difficulty disappeared instantly. She trembled and shook quite often during Communion. Afterward she quieted down; at such times, she sat
quietly and listened to prayer. On the other hand, evenings
following days of Communion were frequently times of
vicious attacks that took place later at night. Those were the
times of Satan's revenge."

The idea that the girl was engaged in some sort of hoax
began to lose ground at the mission station, particularly when
it was noted that she suffered great discomfort during the
possession states. Repeatedly, Father Hörner's report to his
superiors noted the incredible speed with which Germana
moved when possessed. Snakelike agility and manner were
also observed. Her levitations were accompanied by unusual
phenomena. She sometimes moved from her bed as if she
were a snake, with her body rubbery. Father Hörner reported
that "sometimes she moved on her back, at other times on
her belly, in snakelike motions" and "when she moved backwards, her head settled on the ground as if it were a foot and
her whole body moved downward, snake fashion." While she
was being exorcised, standing up, those present noted that
Germana's neck elongated, so that it looked like a snake.

On one occasion, while a nun was kneeling before her,
Germana darted down in what Father Hörner called "a typical snake manner" and bit the nun's arm where it was covered by her habit. Where the girls' teeth had left their mark,
a reddish point showed at the center and a small wound re-
sembling a snake bite emerged. The girl was also credited
with being able to run up a wall, two yards high, with such
speed that "it seemed she was moving on solid ground."

The girl's suffering was divided by her exorcist into three
major physiological categories: (1) Swellings: "The wicked
enemy plagued the poor girl horribly. The veins on her forehead stood out frighteningly. Neck, head, and left shoulder
and arms were also quite swollen, so that it looked as if the
veins might burst. Germana, at such times, used to crouch

forward and whimper like a dying person, while her face was ashen gray." (2) Peculiar sounds: "No animal had ever made such sounds, neither the lions of East Africa nor angry bulls. At times it sounded as if a veritable herd of wild beasts, orchestrated by Satan, had formed a hellish choir. There was howling, barking, hissing, growling, owl-like sounds, hyenalike noises, and all this mixed with the thundering, cursing, and wailing of a human voice. All these sounds could not possibly have been created by a human being." (3) An uncanny glitter in Germana's eyes prompted Father Hörner to write that "the eyes of the possessed burned with an inhuman fire that prompted the onlooker to experience hot and cold shivers."

The phenomena around the girl were not limited to insistent and untraceable poundings at doors. The sound of horses' hoofs was also heard. The exorcist said "we heard the sound of rapidly approaching horses," on returning to the missing station, "which created havoc among the travelers. Everyone yelled, and people ran in all directions, but when we looked back, there was nothing to be seen." On another occasion, Father Hörner states, "the heavy sound of passing horses could be heard overtaking us, but again nothing was to be seen." He reports that a sound was heard that "suggested something falling off the roof, but there was no visual cause." Seemingly quite exhausted by all these phenomena, the confessor-exorcist concludes this part of his report, "Well, there was a good deal of this sort of thing."

Just what the Germana phenomena did to the mental state of the other people at the mission station is difficult to imagine. Whether it was connected with the possession case or not, one of the nuns reported that she saw a charming kitten on a bench, but when she went to pet it, the cat turned into "a gigantic black dog, as big as a calf, with glittering fiery eyes." She told Hörner that she heard a sound, like thunder, and the creature disappeared. Nuns and girls reported seeing apparitions of frogs and toads, outside their windows, "some big and some small (some larger than a human hand), their eyes fiery and protruding." These images disappeared after five to ten minutes. When they went outside the house, "nothing could be seen, but we could hear taunting laughter all around us." Frogs also played a part in an incident that involved the possessed girl and her exorcist. Father Hörner's report relates the following details:

"One morning Germana said, laughing, 'Look under the altar box!' I did not follow her suggestion but realized that she kept glancing at it with such fear that I was reminded of a snake that used to come to the house quite frequently. To my amazement, some fifty or so frogs had managed to enter the box. She did not permit anyone to touch the reptiles but put them into a container and had them thrown down a hole, far away from the altar. But by midday the same number had assembled once more. I had them also removed. This time, however, when no one was looking, I had a medal placed within the altar. Now there was no recurrence of the phenomenon; peace had returned."

As her exorcist, we have noted, Father Hörner had difficulty separating Germana's identity from that of the possessing Devil. Nor is it clear from his report whether the girl actually experienced amnesia during the possession periods. Although authorities on possession say that this state is unlike that of an hypnotic or mediumistic trance, some of Germana's actions suggest a trancelike condition, at least now and then. At times, she walked back and forth, talking to herself but seemingly oblivious of what she was doing. When she was asked to keep quiet, the Devil within her said, "No one can command me! This is not Germana, but Satan; I, the one who inhabits her, now speaks to you. Germana knows nothing of this."

Experiments in halting the possession with drugs were unsuccessful. When she was given sedative tablets, Germana laughed and exclaimed, "Well, so the long-legged fool has given me medicines to make me sleep! But has anyone ever been able to put a spirit to sleep?" The tablets had no effect, and the girl carried on for hours. She was also, like some hypnotized subjects, able to ignore pain while in a possession state. Germana was fully aware of this and said, "You can burn me or cut me and do whatever you like. But when I am in this condition, I just don't feel a thing. Later on, though, when I am my own self again, then I will be in pain."

The ultimate success of the exorcism may be linked to the tradition of which Germana was a part, and of her life story before she joined the mission. Her full name was Clara Germana Cele, and she was a native of Natal. Her parents were converts to Roman Catholicism, and the child was baptized while she was a minor. Her stay at the mission began, as we have seen, at the age of four. But when she was six or seven years old, the girl was reported to have been "seduced sexually" by a "woman magician." She lived with other children for ten years afterwards, and nothing emotionally unusual was noticed about her until the possession symptoms and her "pact with the Devil" became known.

Permission to perform an exorcism on Germana, to rid her of diabolical possession, was issued by the local Bishop's office on September 10, 1906. Father Erasmus Hörner was assisted in the rite by the house father of the mission, Father Mansuet. As in all exorcisms, the diabolical entity was first asked to identify itself and gave several names, such as "Yiminia" and either "Balek" or "Malek." When pressed for accuracy, the Devil replied, "We do not all have names. Only the important ones have names, not those that are insignificant. I am small and insignificant."

Exorcism rites took place on the first morning, ending by noon, and beginning again by 3 P.M. The procedure lasted late into the night. The next day, the rite was continued from 8 to 10 A.M. There were several hopeful days, and a number of setbacks. When, the following January, Father Erasmus Hörner made plans to go to Europe, Germana asked him to postpone the trip. He was unable to do so. In his absence, the girl experienced a relapse; in fact, she announced that she had made a new pact with the Devil.

The Apostolic Vicar, Dr. Henri Delalle, Bishop of Natal, paid a visit to the mission to make sure that Germana's possession was genuine. Accompanied by Father Delagues, O.M.I., the bishop made a first-hand check of the girl's condition and confirmed that possession was, indeed, in effect. A new exorcism began on April 24, 1907. Although the attending priests were at times discouraged, Germana insisted that the exorcism be continued. At last, the Devil departed, leaving a stench "that could not be compared with anything else." Germana lived a normal mission life until her death of tuberculosis on March 14, 1912, at the age of twenty-three.

SELECTED BIBLIOGRAPHY

Balducci, Corrado. *Gli indemoniati*. Rome, 1959.

Blatty, William Peter. *The Exorcist*. New York: Harper & Row, 1971.

De Jesus-Marie, Bruno, ed. *Satan*. New York: Sheed and Ward, 1952.

Ebon, Martin. *Exorcism: Fact, not Fiction*. New York: New American Library, 1976.

————. *The Devil's Bride: Exorcism, Past and Present*. New York: Harper & Row, 1975.

————. *The Satan Trap: Dangers of the Occult*. New York: Doubleday, 1976.

Kelly, Henry Ansgar. *The Devil, Demonology and Witchcraft*. New York: Doubleday, 1968.

Oesterreich, T. K. *Possession: Demoniacal and Other*. New Hyde Park, N.Y.: University Books, 1966.

Petitpierre, Dom Robert, ed. *Exorcism: The Findings of a Commission Convened by the Bishop of Exeter*. London: S.P.C.K., 1972.

Rodewyk, Adolf. *Possessed by Satan*. New York: Doubleday, 1975.

Rogo, D. Scott. *Parapsychology: A Century of Inquiry*. New York: Taplinger, 1975.

Roll, W.G., *The Poltergeist*. New York: New American Library, 1972.

Seth, Ronald. *Children Against Witches*. New York: Taplinger, 1969.

Vogl, Carl. *Begone Satan!* Rockford, Ill.: Tan Books, 1973.

Wickland, Carl A. *Thirty Years Among the Dead.* Los Angeles, 1924.

Young, Samuel H. *Psychic Children.* New York: Doubleday, 1977.

About the Author

Martin Ebon served for twelve years as Administrative Secretary of the Parapsychology Foundation and subsequently as a consultant to the Foundation for Research on the Nature of Man. He conducted a series of lectures on "Parapsychology: From Magic to Science" at the New School for Social Research in New York City and has lectured widely, throughout the United States, at institutes of higher learning. Mr. Ebon has edited such periodicals as *Tomorrow,* the *International Journal of Parapsychology,* and *Spiritual Frontiers,* organ of the Spiritual Frontiers Fellowship.

Mr. Ebon's articles and reviews have appeared in a variety of periodicals, ranging from *Contemporary Psychology* to the *U.S. Naval Institute Proceedings.* Some thirty of his books have been published by NAL alone. Among them are THE EVIDENCE FOR LIFE AFTER DEATH; ATLANTIS: THE NEW EVIDENCE; THE RIDDLE OF THE BERMUDA TRIANGLE; and EXORCISM: FACT NOT FICTION.